# HE PULLED HER INTO KISSING RANGE—

and Janet struggled to free herself, pounding ineffectually against his broad chest. "Let me go! Let me go, I tell you. . . ."

"I will not! I warned you what would happen." He caught a hank of her flaming hair and pulled her toward him. "New rules, honey, and a different playground." His other hand ran possessively down her soft curved figure. "And if you only knew how long I've been waiting to get you on this playground, my love. . . ." His voice trailed off as his mouth moved to fasten on her parted lips as if he'd never let them go.

And suddenly Janet wasn't fighting it anymore, for now she knew that she had been waiting for him to hold her and kiss her like this from the moment they first met. . . .

## Other SIGNET Books by Glenna Finley

- [ ] **BRIDAL AFFAIR** (#Q6777—95¢)
- [ ] **JOURNEY TO LOVE** (#Y6773—$1.25)
- [ ] **KISS A STRANGER** (#Q6175—95¢)
- [ ] **LOVE IN DANGER** (#Q6177—95¢)
- [ ] **LOVE'S HIDDEN FIRE** (#Q6171—95¢)
- [ ] **LOVE LIES NORTH** (#Q6017—95¢)
- [ ] **LOVE'S MAGIC SPELL** (#Y6778—$1.25)
- [ ] **A PROMISING AFFAIR** (#Y6776—$1.25)
- [ ] **THE RELUCTANT MAIDEN** (#Y6781—$1.25)
- [ ] **THE ROMANTIC SPIRIT** (#Y6774—$1.25)
- [ ] **SURRENDER MY LOVE** (#Y6775—$1.25)
- [ ] **TREASURE OF THE HEART** (#Q6090—95¢)
- [ ] **WHEN LOVE SPEAKS** (#Q6181—95¢)

---

**THE NEW AMERICAN LIBRARY, INC.,**
P.O. Box 999, Bergenfield, New Jersey 07621

Please send me the SIGNET BOOKS I have checked above. I am enclosing $_____(check or money order—no currency or C.O.D.'s). Please include the list price plus 25¢ a copy to cover handling and mailing costs. (Prices and numbers are subject to change without notice.)

Name_____

Address_____

City_____State_____Zip Code_____
Allow at least 3 weeks for delivery

# THE CAPTURED HEART

*by*
*Glenna Finley*

A SIGNET BOOK
NEW AMERICAN LIBRARY
TIMES MIRROR

SIGNET AND MENTOR BOOKS ARE ALSO AVAILABLE AT DISCOUNTS IN BULK QUANTITY FOR INDUSTRIAL OR SALES-PROMOTIONAL USE. FOR DETAILS, WRITE TO PREMIUM MARKETING DIVISION, NEW AMERICAN LIBRARY, INC., 1301 AVENUE OF THE AMERICAS, NEW YORK, NEW YORK 10019.

COPYRIGHT © 1975 BY GLENNA FINLEY

All rights reserved

SIGNET TRADEMARK REG. U.S. PAT. OFF. AND FOREIGN COUNTRIES
REGISTERED TRADEMARK—MARCA REGISTRADA
HECHO EN CHICAGO, U.S.A.

SIGNET, SIGNET CLASSICS, MENTOR, PLUME AND MERIDIAN BOOKS are published by The New American Library, Inc., 1301 Avenue of the Americas, New York, New York 10019

FIRST PRINTING, AUGUST, 1975

1 2 3 4 5 6 7 8 9

PRINTED IN THE UNITED STATES OF AMERICA

*For Duncan*

"To capture a woman
First, capture her heart"

—*Polynesian proverb*

# Chapter One

Scott Frazier caught his first glance of the young woman when he stepped onto the crowded Kailua pier from the charter boat after a frustrating morning angling for marlin. During the hours he'd spent offshore when the big fish were ignoring his bait, he'd had plenty of time to admire Hawaii's rugged coastline. Now, he decided, it was a pleasure to see some softer curves.

The woman in question was a gorgeous redhead in her early twenties with a matte-finish complexion that rated stares in a part of the U. S. where suntans were the rule rather than the exception. Her hair was tied back with a scarf in a casual ponytail out of deference to the heat, but the simple style enhanced a small, straight nose and features that could have graced a high-fashion cover. Scott's glance moved lazily past her high cheekbones to delicate lips and then on to the softer curves which had first attracted his attention.

They were still there, though discreetly revealed, under a sleeveless navy blue blouse and pleated white skirt. The skirt especially earned his approval with a hemline short enough to display a pair of sensational legs and ankles. He smiled without being aware of it and let his glance wander upward once again.

This time, all he got for his trouble was an unobstructed view of the back of the girl's head as she avoided the throngs of Aloha Week enthusiasts and lingered at the edge of the pier to stare at the famed Kailua-Kona coastline.

There was no question that the view rated a second look. The line of luxury hotels extended for miles; every point of land jutting into the water was crowned with a lofty contemporary structure like the king row on a checkerboard. And each hotel faithfully copied its neighbor with a matching honeycomb of lanai railings and balconies.

But no one could criticize the spectacular scenery behind the coastal developments. Hawaii's terrain ranged steadily upward in a series of plateaus with thick vegetation cloaking the big island in shades of green until it vanished under puffy gray clouds at the cone of Hualalai. The air at the dormant volcano's 8,000-foot summit was undoubtedly chilly, but sweltering heat made a mockery of autumn's temperatures on the Kona coast.

# THE CAPTURED HEART

Scott felt a trickle of perspiration run down his back and decided the sun was too hot even for the pleasant sport of girl-watching.

By then, the young woman was checking the name on the stern of the charter boat against the letter she was holding in her hand. Her glance slid over the craft's deserted deck until it reached the gangway where she encountered Scott's amused stare. She flushed and looked down at the letter again, obviously loathe to query his identity until she was sure.

Scott calmly shed the pullover sweater he'd needed out on the water and decided to make Janet Frazier take the initiative. "She's a redhead," one of the senior partners in his law firm had written, "so you shouldn't have any trouble recognizing her. Judge Byrne is honorary chairman of that Oriental Fine Arts Exhibit that's touring the U.S. mainland this winter and he sent her to Hawaii for an advance look at it. Miss Frazier has taken a leave of absence as the Judge's court coordinator to help him with this tour. I told him you were over there combining business and pleasure this month and that you'd be glad to keep an eye on the girl."

Scott's reaction to that paragraph had been a derisive snort. Shepherding a dewy-eyed arts lover around in his spare time was a hell of a note! Now that she'd appeared on the scene, he remembered that they'd met in the Judge's chambers two years before. That time they'd had a battle royal over some trivial procedure and parted with no love lost.

3

His eyes kindled as he thought about it. Certainly he wasn't going to change his mind about the woman now just because she was more decorative than he'd remembered. There were plenty of good-looking women in Hawaii but marlin were definitely scarce. If Janet Frazier thought he was going to give up the best sports fishing in the Pacific to usher her around some displays of Ming porcelain, she had another think coming!

He saw the redhead give him another fleeting glance before pulling a pair of sunglasses from the top of her head and settling them on her nose. Then, as if having donned additional armor, she moved purposefully toward him.

Scott stayed where he was. He was amused to see that Miss Frazier didn't look enchanted at the prospect of renewing his acquaintance either.

He was right about that. In fact, he would have been chagrined to know that Janet's reaction had been equally abhorrent when she'd received Judge Byrne's letter telling her to contact a lawyer in Kona who would have to be pried away from a marlin rod. That was bad enough. Now, as her memories of Scott Frazier started to crystallize, it was worse than ever. She decided there should be a law against tall, rangy men in their thirties whose broad shoulders and even features had been attracting feminine interest since they'd left their cradles.

The months since their last encounter obviously hadn't diminished Scott's attraction; rather it was intensified with the contrast of his sandy hair against his deeply tanned skin. When she recalled his stern jawline and a pair of disconcertingly critical gray eyes under thick brows, it was no wonder she hesitated approaching him.

Those same eyebrows were drawing together in a puzzled line as she came up beside him, hooding his expression so that it didn't give anything away.

"Mr. Frazier?" Janet made her voice crisp. "Perhaps you remember me?"

"Yes indeed, Miss Frazier. We agreed to disagree in lower Manhattan one day." His tone was deep and equally businesslike but his mouth showed his amusement. He watched her complexion change color before he went on. "I see you received a letter, too."

She nodded. "From Judge Byrne. . . ."

"I thought so. Probably our respective bosses decided we needed to form a mutual assistance pact. Or maybe they thought we were shirttail relatives and should be reunited."

Her chin went up defensively. "That's hardly likely. My father's name was Smith. Unfortunately, he died when I was a baby and I only became a Frazier after my mother's remarriage in Illinois years later."

"And my family's from Connecticut so we're not even kissing kin. It's too bad, but I imagine we'll both survive." He sidestepped to get out of the way of a group of Aloha Week revelers who were beginning to congregate on the pier.

His careless comment prompted Janet to look more

disapproving than ever. She settled her sunglasses firmly on her nose as she said, "I don't want to keep you from your own plans any longer, Mr. Frazier. It's been nice meeting you again. I'll give your best to Judge Byrne when I see him. . . ."

"Hold on there . . ." Scott caught her elbow in an iron grip when she started to turn and walk away. "Not so fast. You're not getting rid of me quite so soon. Not after all the work that's gone into getting us together."

She made a halfhearted attempt to get loose. "I don't know what you mean. This certainly wasn't *my* idea."

For some strange reason, Scott found her pronouncement annoying. It was especially ironic since his own feelings had paralleled hers until she put it in words. "You've made that abundantly clear," he said in a stiff tone. "Unfortunately things are beyond our control at this point." As she stared uncomprehendingly up at him, he went on. "I have a letter, too . . . from my boss. He and Judge Byrne have decided I'm to keep an eye on you while you're over here."

Janet's lips formed an uncompromising line. "That's utterly ridiculous. I'm twenty-three years old and I certainly don't need anyone to hold my hand."

"I wouldn't think of it," Scott assured her. Right then, the only reason he would have been tempted to capture one of those slim white hands would be to make sure she didn't throw an uppercut at him. From her angry expression it was obviously in her mind.

# THE CAPTURED HEART

"Simmer down, Miss Frazier. I'm not any more thrilled by this than you are."

"That thought *did* cross my mind," Janet told him, attempting to regain a measure of her poise. She firmly believed in equal rights between the sexes but she'd never had any man treat her in such a negligible fashion. She sniffed audibly and chose a reasonable tone which she knew would infuriate him. "It's quite simple really. We've both done our part . . . now all we have to do is write a couple of letters ourselves. I'll tell the Judge everything is fine and you tell your senior partner that we met but I didn't have time to fit you into my schedule."

Her calm dismissal brought a surge of red to Scott's thin cheeks that didn't have anything to do with his morning's sunburn. "Well, I'll be damned," he said softly. "You'd better come back down to earth with the rest of us mortals, Miss Frazier. I have no intention of messing up your precious schedule but I'm also not going to let myself in for a broadside by not following orders. Senior partners of law firms don't like to have their dictates ignored." He eyed her sourly. "Although if your precious Judge is so worried over your health, why in hell didn't he come over and hold your hand himself."

Janet's glance fell at that. "He planned to," she admitted. "He and his wife were both coming but Mrs. Byrne sprained his wrist two weeks ago and she didn't feel like traveling."

"So you came alone?"

"Of course. The Exhibit dates can't be postponed and the Judge will have a fit if anything goes wrong on the mainland tour. He feels pretty strongly about it."

"And if I know Judge Byrne—that's an understatement." Scott sighed and rubbed his chin wearily. "So let's not have any more chatter about your doing it all alone."

"Oh, for heaven's sake—it isn't that bad." Janet flipped a graphic hand toward the throngs on the crowded pier. "I'm not in the middle of Siberia or the Sahara Desert. This is Hawaii . . . and I don't have to get my money changed."

"Just make sure that you brought enough of it," he conceded.

Her lips curved in response. "I've already found that out. I spent an hour in the Honolulu airport when I changed planes."

"Okay . . . so we're in agreement on one thing." He shoved his hands in the pockets of his cotton slacks as he surveyed her. "There's no reason why we can't compromise on the rest. Are you staying here in Kona?"

She shook her head. "No . . . at a hotel called Kaiulani up at the north end of the island." Her forehead wrinkled. "Or maybe it's south. I've been mixed up ever since I landed a little while ago."

"It's north," Scott told her, his voice softening perceptibly. "And if you just got to the Islands, I'm not surprised that you're hot and bothered. It's a long flight from Manhattan . . . even with a layover."

"Maybe that's why this seems so unreal." Janet looked around the pier again. "I feel I've flown straight into a South Seas travelogue. There was frost when I left home but it was over ninety when I changed planes in Honolulu ten hours later."

"Don't think the Hawaiian Chamber of Commerce hasn't publicized that fact," Scott told her with a grin. "By tomorrow, you'll have shed your nylons and gone native just like them." He jerked his head toward two bikini-clad girls who were sauntering up the gangway to talk to the crew on a sports fishing boat anchored alongside.

Janet rubbed her hot forehead with the back of her hand. "If I last that long."

"You'll find it's cooler up the coast at Kaiulani. Actually we're in luck . . ."

"What do you mean?" She was trying to match her steps to his longer ones as they strolled down the pier.

"I'm moving up there today, as well. Once we're in the same hotel, all we have to do is compare notes over a drink now and then and we'll satisfy everybody at home. How about it?"

Janet was surprised to find that his offhand solution made her more annoyed than ever. "Oh, fine," she told him through clenched teeth. "Just dandy. They have a lot of boats in here, haven't they," she went on, trying to sound as if the subject fascinated her. "What's that greenery on the top of that one?"

"Ti leaves." A faint smile crossed his face. "These fishermen don't take any chances. Practically every one of them ties some ti leaves to the wheelhouse roof before they set out for marlin."

"For luck?"

He nodded. "Hawaiians believe to a man that the ti leaf holds a power for sailors . . . just the way they know that bananas aboard the boat mean trouble. Only don't ask them to explain it." He rubbed his neck. "Somebody must have packed a banana in his lunch by mistake this morning. We didn't have a strike all the time we were out."

Their steps slowed as they came alongside a weather-beaten tug which was tying up beyond the part of the pier reserved for skin-diving expeditions.

Janet copied his impersonal tone as she surveyed it. "That can't be used for sports fishing—it looks as if it's been around since Captain Cook's days."

Scott pulled up to squint at the rusty deck plates. "It must be used for inter-island work . . . probably on some of the barges over there."

"What do they haul on those?"

"Everything that costs too much to transport by air." Scott gave the Eurasian crew coming down the nearest barge gangway a cursory look.

Janet, with feminine interest in detail, let her glance linger longer. She was especially intrigued by the different facial characteristics of the two young women who made their way easily down the steep gangway despite the narrow pale blue cheong-sams they were wearing. The first girl exhibited a voluptuous South Seas figure with black hair cascading to her shoulders. The girl behind her looked diminutive by contrast and wore her shiny dark hair cropped close in a Dutch bob. She scurried past them, keeping her glance at shoe-top level, but her companion favored Scott with an openly appraising and inviting stare.

Scott started to grin before intercepting Janet's disdainful grimace. He looked as if he'd like to comment on it but contented himself by saying, "Why the sudden interest in Hawaiian economy?"

"I'm not the only one," she replied, stung by his amusement. "Look at all the people on this pier."

Then he did burst out laughing. "They haven't come to admire the boats. The parade forms here for Aloha Week festivities. There's an investiture at the Hulihee Palace. It used to be a summer residence for Hawaiian royalty," he added in an offhand manner.

"So that's the reason for those people in the capes and feather headdresses." Janet was watching some brightly costumed Polynesians get in line behind a young Hawaiian boy who was wearing only a patterned loincloth.

Scott nodded. "Those men and women are royalty from the other islands. That youngster blows on a big conch shell to clear their way through town. The old gentleman draped in the sheet at the rear is one of the honored elders at the ceremony." Scott looked at his watch. "We'll be parboiled if we stand out in this sun any longer. It's a good thing my car is air-conditioned and parked at the end of the pier. We can pick up your luggage on the way out of town."

"Pick up my luggage . . ." she repeated dazedly before hurrying to catch up with him. "Just a minute . . . I . . . I don't understand. Where are you going?"

"We," he corrected briskly. "We might as well go straight along to Kaiulani now. I think an earlier arrival would suit you. As soon as you have some rest you'll look better."

His casual comment indicated she had considerable room for improvement. An attitude, she could have told him, which no man had mentioned to her before. She ignored the perspiration trickling down her back and announced stiffly, "I feel fine right now. Besides, I believe the hotel furnishes a bus or a limousine this afternoon. They're expecting to pick me up and I'd rather keep to my itinerary."

None of Scott's varied female acquaintances had ever preferred an unknown bus driver to him. It was evident in the way he stared at her. "Whatever you say. You could cancel the arrangement, but I certainly don't want to insist. If you prefer to wait for the hotel bus . . ." He shrugged broad shoulders eloquently. "Have at it."

Janet decided belatedly that she might have been more tactful. "It was very kind of you to offer . . ." She paused to move out of the way of three men wearing convention badges who were staggering drunken-

# THE CAPTURED HEART

ly down the pier. "They'll fall into the water if they get too close to the edge."

"Might sober 'em up," Scott said callously. "But if you feel they need a chaperone, go ahead and volunteer. You have a couple hours before it's time for the bus."

Her chin came up. "I plan to watch the parade and look through the shops." She managed a polite little smile. "Don't let me keep you. I imagine we'll see each other now and then at Kaiulani."

Scott translated that to "but not if I see you first." His eyes glinted with annoyance. "I'm sure we will, Miss Frazier. Just one last word of advice . . ."

"Yes." The monosyllable didn't hold any encouragement.

"I'd suggest you get in the shade during some of the parade. Otherwise you'll be out of commission for a day or so. Your face is red already."

"It's kind of you to be concerned . . ." she began stiffly.

"Which means that you're madder than hell." He hitched up his slacks and bestowed a mirthless smile. "I can see where you come by that red hair naturally."

"If you think I'm going to stand here and listen to a lecture . . ."

"Calm down, honey, I'm on my way." His gray eyes turned glacial. "In the meantime, don't be a stubborn little fool. Do as you're told, or I'll wring that beautiful neck the next time I see you."

13

After that autocratic pronouncement he strode down the pier without looking back. He had shouldered through the parade participants and was out of sight before Janet could think of a properly scathing reply. She deliberately took another turn around the pier, pretending an interest in her surroundings while she decided to ignore her meeting with him. If Judge Byrne should inquire, she would . . . Her mind went blank. Would what? Admit that she had come off second-best in a go-round with Scott Frazier. Definitely not.

She tried to remember what she'd heard about him on the legal grapevine. He was a promising corporate lawyer; the Judge had told her that when he'd noticed their identical surnames. He'd even mentioned the old established law firm Scott had just joined.

She frowned as she went on to remember what had been said about his personal life. Nothing that she could recall. Which meant that he was either discreet or simply did nothing to cause comment. Janet thought again of the man who had just disappeared down the pier and decided to be honest. Scott Frazier was discreet. Obviously any move he made would cause comment as far as women were concerned.

Possibly that was why the Judge had decided to play a heavy-handed Cupid. It wouldn't be the first time he and Mrs. Byrne had tried to direct her social life. Probably they'd be asking how she and Scott were getting along in their first telephone call and she'd have to be ready with an evasive answer. Cer-

## THE CAPTURED HEART

tainly she couldn't say that she planned to avoid the man in the future and that Scott was planning exactly the same maneuver to make it unanimous.

So much for the Byrnes's romantic hopes! She rubbed her moist temple with a weary hand and closed her eyes for an instant behind the dark lenses. If only it weren't so hot! A quick glance at her watch showed that she had two more hours before the hotel bus was due to pick her up. Obviously she'd have to find a shady spot before that or Scott's high-handed prognosis would turn out to be right. She pushed her way through the crowd of people now starting to line the main street for the parade. Perhaps if she wandered through the grounds of the Hulihee Palace, she could find a bench in the shade.

She strolled along the sidewalk, glancing apathetically at the displays of Hawaiian souvenirs crammed into every store window. Shell necklaces, brightly colored muu-muus and aloha shirts vied with macadamia nuts, coconut chips, and Kona coffee for counter space. Any other time, she would have been as eager as the other visitors thronging the shops. Now, she was simply too hot and tired to care. The realization that she could have been sitting in air-conditioned comfort while being driven to Kaiulani didn't improve her disposition.

The palace was across the street from an impressive coral and lava building which she discovered was the original Christian church in the Islands. It was a closer refuge, but a large tour bus was just pulling up in front of it ready to disgorge an eager group of visitors. Janet took another look and prudently detoured into the Palace entrance.

She waited behind a pair of young honeymooners who were paying their admission fees. A dignified gray-haired Hawaiian lady gave them their tickets and urged them not to miss the Aloha Week investiture to be held in the grounds later on.

As the couple passed her, Janet heard the bride asking her husband, "What's this Aloha Week?"

He looked stricken for a moment and then said confidently, "It's sort of like the Fourth of July or Armistice Day. Same idea, anyway."

Janet's amused glance met that of the Hawaiian hostess. They waited until the honeymooners disappeared through a door to the grounds before starting to laugh.

"Why won't a man ever ask?" the hostess said, shaking her head in dismay as she accepted Janet's entrance fee. "Or better still, admit to his wife that there's something he doesn't know?"

"Beats me," Janet grinned. "You can satisfy *my* curiosity though. What *is* Aloha Week?"

"These days, simply an opportunity to show the visitors a glimpse of Hawaiian music and culture," the woman admitted. "In ancient times, this season was the *Makahiki*, the months when war and work were discarded. Our chiefs collected taxes for Lono, God of the Harvest. If the people gave their share of fruits of the land and sea, then they were assured of four months of peace. War was forbidden, work was *pau* . . ."

"Pau?"

"Finished," the other explained. "It was all play and feasting. Sounds like a fairy tale nowadays, doesn't it?" Then she smiled and said, "Don't miss the feather cloaks and helmets on display in the room to the right."

Janet nodded her thanks and started her tour of the well-kept mansion. Between the exhibits inside and the parade festivities which culminated on the palace grounds, time passed more quickly than she planned and she finally had to hurry to get back to the pier for her drive up the island.

Her transportation turned out to be a late-model station wagon with the name Kaiulani boldly outlined by a painted Hawaiian flower lei on the side of it. A slim Eurasian in his early twenties who wore a cheerful smile along with his violent aloha shirt greeted her as she paused on the curb.

"Going to the Kaiulani, ma'am?"

"I hope so. My name's Janet Frazier. Am I on your list?"

He fished a paper from his shirt pocket and consulted it. "You bet. How about Mr. Frazier?" he asked, leaning over to open the front door of the station wagon for her.

Janet frowned. "He went on ahead in his own car. Why? Was he supposed to be on this trip?"

The young man pursed his lips, the grimace looking strange under his carefully trimmed mandarin moustache. "The hotel people weren't sure. It's hard to keep things straight when most of our reservations are made from the mainland. It doesn't matter though. I had to bring some guests in earlier for a flight to Maui. I think I saw you on the pier then."

"Probably. I was interested in watching the boats and the people."

He grinned and flipped his hand toward the still-crowded jetty. "What's so different about this? I thought it was pretty run-of-the-mill."

"The docks on the Hudson River don't specialize in rusty tugs or girls wearing cheong-sams." She smiled disarmingly. "Believe me, I was impressed by the scenery here."

"So long as we keep our tourists happy." He glanced over his shoulder as if suddenly remembering he had work to do. "Is your luggage around?"

"Why yes. Those two tweed ones with a suede trim." She indicated them stacked at the curb.

"I'll load them in a minute. Go ahead and get in the car," he urged her. "We'll be on our way in no time."

Janet did as he suggested and hastily rolled down the window of the station wagon to take advantage of the faint afternoon breeze that was stirring. Despite the driver's promise, it was a full ten minutes before he reappeared, talking to a couple in their mid-thirties who were wearing leis around their necks and carrying still more bags. The partially bald man was wearing a sports shirt and had his pants tucked into cowboy boots while his wife was in a bare-midriff slack outfit with her bleached blonde hair worn long and straight.

"Sorry to keep you waiting," the driver said to Janet as he opened the rear door of the stationwagon, "but I found these people looking for a ride to Kaiulani, too."

"I didn't know we were holding things up," the man said, ushering his wife ahead of him into the car. "I'm Martin Bristow . . . this is my wife, Bonita."

"But everybody calls me Bunny," the blonde put in cheerfully.

"I'm Janet Frazier." She smiled at them over her shoulder. "Did you just arrive?"

Bunny nodded, yawning. "From Jersey City by way of L. A. and Disneyland. Why didn't somebody tell me America was so big. I'm dead . . . absolutely dead."

Her husband gave her an anxious look. "I keep telling you . . . you can sleep all winter when we get back to Jersey. Besides, it can't be much farther now to this place . . . Kaiulani. Is that right?" he queried the driver when the young man slid in the front seat and started the car.

"About fifty miles," the other replied.

Bonita Bristow gave a slight moan.

"Cheer up," her husband told her. "At least you can relax here. She never closes an eye on airplanes," he confided to the other two. "Spends all her time watching the wings to make sure the jets are still there."

"Well, you don't have to worry now, Mrs. Bristow," their driver said, directing his grin toward the rear-view mirror. "Once we get out of Kona, our road's practically bare so you couldn't be safer."

"Then I'll take a little nap if you're sure I won't miss anything." Bunny Bristow started to remove her lei but leaned forward to ask their driver, "What's your name?"

"Rodney Kahori, ma'am. Rod . . . for short."

"Okay, Rod," she said amiably, "Wake me up if there's something interesting to see. After coming this far . . . well, you know how it is. I might not be back."

"You bet, Mrs. Bristow." He stopped at a busy intersection and then gunned the accelerator as they turned onto a highway which climbed steeply before leaving the Kailua coast.

The lush tropical foliage and plantings continued for a few miles as they drove through suburban residential areas but eventually thinned as the road cut away from the water and headed inland.

Rod Kahori hummed to himself as he handled the car easily in the thin traffic on the two-lane road.

Bonita closed her eyes before they reached Kailua-Kona's city limits and her long hair fell forward to shield her face as she leaned against her husband's shoulder. He grinned and winked at Janet as she gave them a shy glance when the car gathered speed.

# THE CAPTURED HEART

"The poor gal's exhausted," he said. "I guess we've tried to do too much. You know that old jazz about the spirit willing but the flesh crying uncle."

"I certainly do." Janet felt an instinctive sympathy for her fellow travelers. Their outfits might be more suited to Hollywood Boulevard or a Cheyenne rodeo but the trappings seemed to cloak two warm-hearted, likable people. She sighed unconsciously as she looked at the countryside which had changed from tropical density to rocky barren reaches as the car climbed to a higher elevation.

"The scenery's pretty dull," Rodney confirmed with a quick sideways glance. "There's not much to see on this trip."

"You mean my wife's the sensible one?" Martin asked.

"Well, the Hamakua Coast north of Hilo on the other side of the island is the scenic way. There's not much along here until you get up to where Kaiulani is. That's ranch country with the mountains and all. Prettiest place in Hawaii," he added proudly. "You'll see!"

"Seems funny to hear you mention ranches over here," Martin said. "Are you talking about cattle?"

"You bet!" Rodney emphasized. "Some of these owners have thousands of acres in their spreads. The big island supplies most of the beef for Hawaii. They used to ship it from the Kona pier." He gave Janet a quick glance. "I meant to ask—was that Mr. Frazier?" Then, as she looked puzzled, he went on. "The fellow you were talking to on the pier. The tall man who came off one of the charter boats."

"Oh, yes." Janet flushed slightly. "You have a good memory." She searched for another topic before Martin Bristow started asking questions, as well. "Have you worked for Kaiulani very long, Rodney?"

"A year or so. My mother got me the job. She's the social director there." He shrugged thin shoulders without taking his glance from the road. "I had to have a steady job after I got married."

Janet stared at him. "Good heavens, you don't look old enough to be married."

He burst out laughing, looking absurdly young despite his theatrical moustache. "Better not tell my wife that. We just celebrated our second anniversary. She's expecting a baby any time now."

"Congratulations!" Martin told him. "You have us beat."

"No children?" Rodney asked.

Martin looked sheepish. "Nope. S'matter of fact . . . we're on sort of a delayed honeymoon. Couldn't get away last summer."

Janet half-turned in the seat to smile at him. "I suppose Mrs. Bristow had to convince you to come to Hawaii?"

"Bunny?" His arm tightened around his wife's shoulders. "Nope. She held out for southern California. Hawaii was my idea."

"You mean you'd heard how great Kaiulani was?" Rodney asked, sounding proprietory.

"Wrong again. I read about the Oriental Fine Arts Exhibit and wanted a look at it before it hit the mainland." He noted their puzzled expressions and grinned. "Don't let the cowboy boots fool you. I'm a washout on a fast draw but I know the way to a seventh-century Indian Buddha like Napoleon knew the road to Waterloo. If some of those exhibits are going up for bids at the end of the tour, I want to get in early."

"There aren't many of them in that category," Janet said.

"Then *you* know about the sale conditions, too." His eyes narrowed thoughtfully as she nodded. When she didn't volunteer any more information, he went on, "I wonder how many other potential buyers are coming here?"

"Enough so that the hotel is crammed full," Rodney put in. "Kaiulani hasn't been so crowded since its grand opening five years ago. I'm surprised you were able to get reservations," he added without rancor. "The front desk turned down a governor and a couple of state senators the other day."

"My reservations were made some time ago," Janet murmured, wishing that Judge Byrne and his wife had come, after all. While she found most Oriental art pieces attractive, she couldn't identify a seventh-century Buddha unless someone took her gently by the hand and pointed it out.

"I hope Bunny will like the place," Martin added.

"She doesn't care much about art exhibits so she's hoping there's a decent beach."

"Wait till you see it," Rodney assured him. "All white sand . . . really beautiful!"

"Looks like there'll have to be a minor miracle between now and then," Martin said, jerking his head toward the desolate landscape of rocks, grass, and prickly pear cactus beyond the car windows. "Nobody told me Hawaii was like this."

"Wait till you see the northern end of the island," Rodney told him, pressing down on the accelerator as if impatient to prove his words. "First we come to the rolling grassland of the ranch country . . . then we drop about two thousand feet to Kaiulani on the coast. It's the prettiest place you could hope to find."

Martin nodded with satisfaction and slouched in the seat. "Then pour on the coal, boy. We can't get there too soon for me."

When Rodney turned off the main road under an arch reading "Kaiulani" an hour later, his passengers could see that he hadn't exaggerated in his praises.

"I've never seen such flowers," marveled Bonita, who had awakened from her nap a few minutes before and was busily staring out the window at the profusion of color on either side of the car. The green fairways of a championship golf course beyond were edged by a bougainvillea covering on low stone boundary fences. Around the next curve, brilliant Flamboyant trees with their scarlet foliage were planted to cloak slender light-poles of contemporary design on the shoulder of the road. Orchids grew thickly at their base along with the glossy-leaved plumeria shrubs whose delicate blossoms perfumed the air.

"Did you ever smell anything so heavenly?" Bunny went on enthusiastically. "I had no idea it would be this nice."

Martin scratched the side of his nose. "You could have fooled me, too."

Rodney turned to check with Janet. "And you, ma'am? What do you think of our island now?"

She smiled at him like a conspirator. "I'm surprised that Adam and Eve ever left. I think if I had something as pretty as this, I'd lock the door and throw away the key."

"Just wait until you see the rest of it," he promised.

They drove past a pro shop for the golf course and two parking lots which were discreetly hedged with thick foliage before entering the curving drive to the main part of the hotel.

The building was starkly contemporary in design and fit into the natural contour of the island's terrain. Following this concept, the architect had utilized an expanse of native stone, wood, and glass blended in a type of construction which let in a full measure of Hawaiian sunshine.

Two young men neatly dressed in white Japanese-style uniforms were beside the station wagon even as Rodney braked, ready to start unloading the luggage.

"Our registration desk's right through there." Rodney gestured past the entrance to an expanse of waxed tile patio. It was dominated by a massive flower arrangement of red anthuriums in a brass bowl that measured fully three feet in diameter. "I hope you enjoy your stay at the hotel."

"Will we see you again?" Janet asked.

"Sure thing. Any time you need any travel arrangements . . . I'm your man. On duty every day."

"Your wife can't approve of that," Martin Bristow told him, idly watching the transfer of their luggage.

"The doctor makes her spend most of her time in bed until the baby comes," the young driver said, looking unhappy suddenly. "With all our medical bills, I have to work seven days a week."

"Well, we'll probably be calling on you," Bonita Bristow told him in her bluff, kindly way. "With this heat, I think I'd like being driven around. Besides," she turned to make a face at her husband, "when you're driving you spend all your time swearing at the other drivers . . . and *that's* no vacation for me."

Martin shrugged good-naturedly. "You heard her," he told Rodney. "We'll be in touch."

"I'm sure I will, too," Janet added. "Thank you for making the trip so interesting on the way up."

"Janet Frazier?" asked a male voice behind her and she turned to find a pleasant man in his late twenties studying her with deference. He was of medium height, deeply tanned with curly brown hair cut short, and wearing a well-fitting khaki Palm Beach

# THE CAPTURED HEART

suit. At her nod, he grinned in relief. "I *thought* that Rodney was bringing you along."

"Never lost a passenger yet." Rodney said with a brief grin. "This is Wayne Marshall, who handles the Kaiulani's publicity," he told Janet before hurrying back to the station wagon.

"Mr. Marshall . . ." Recognition lighted Janet's features. "Then you're the man . . ."

". . . who's written you and Judge Byrne all those letters," he confirmed with a nod. "I'm sorry the Byrnes couldn't come, but I'm glad you made it," he added, taking her arm and steering her through the beautiful patio into a roofed section where some rattan couches and chairs were grouped in front of a registration counter. "This art exhibit is attracting more attention than we ever imagined. The hotel's bursting at the seams now and there's a waiting list a yard long. As things stand, we have an ambassador as well as the governor for the opening festivities this weekend."

"If it does half as well on the mainland, there'll be a lot of happy charities," Janet murmured. She was admiring the spacious sunny lobby where a cluster of palms was planted near a massive glass wall. "I think part of the success must be due to your hotel. This is the most gorgeous place I've ever seen." She waved and nodded to the Bristows as they turned away from the registration desk and started to follow a white-jacketed bellboy to their room.

"Friends of yours?" Wayne asked.

"I just met them on the trip from Kona. Martin and Bonita Bristow," she explained. "He's an Oriental art buff here for the display, too."

"I'll have to see if there's anything for a story there," Wayne said, pulling an envelope from his coat pocket and jotting their names on it.

Janet stared at him, puzzled. "But we're so far away from things here. Who'd be interested?"

Wayne Marshall burst out laughing and then sobered as he saw she was in earnest. "Sorry. I forgot you're not used to the Islands. We're getting tremendous coverage in the Honolulu papers already and they're feeding the wire services for mainland distribution." He gave her a cocky grin. "I'll bet you'll be interested in today's paper yourself. Sorry I don't have a copy with me but I'll make sure you get one." He glanced at his watch and then rubbed his jaw. "Damn! It's later than I thought. There are some letters for the last mail pickup so I'll have to run. Probably you'll be glad to rest, anyway. I'm at your service if there's anything I can do to help you. Just give me a call."

Janet felt a touch of panic. "I *did* hope you could furnish an idea of the space needs for the Exhibit. I'd like to make some rough diagrams before the display officially opens."

"Oh, there's plenty of time for that. We have a couple of days before the final stuff arrives and we start uncrating. The insurance people prefer that we leave things until the last minute. Makes their security coverage easier." He beckoned to a heavy-set Hawaiian lady in a dark muu-muu standing by the registration desk. "Janet, this is Thelma Kahori, our social director and hostess," he went on. "She knows as much about you and the Judge Byrne correspondence files as I do."

"How do you do, Mrs. Kahori. I've already met your son—he drove us up from Kona," Janet said, impressed by the older woman's appearance.

The social director had classic features in a broad face and wore her gray hair coiled neatly atop her head. She was taller than her son, with her demeanor reflecting a Polynesian heritage rather than Rodney's more impassively Oriental one.

Thelma smiled. "Rodney just told me. May I show you to your room now or does Wayne have something else planned?"

"Take her along, Thelma. I've explained that we can get together tomorrow." He sneaked another quick look at his watch and grimaced. "Must run. Great to meet you at last, Janet."

The two women watched him hurry off past a gleaming brass Buddha on his way to a corridor flanking the reception desk.

Thelma sighed and shook her head. "Poor Wayne . . . he seldom catches up. You never saw a man work so hard." She smiled at Janet. "If you'll wait just a minute . . . I have something to give you."

"Of course." Janet saw the woman go behind the reception desk and disappear through a door near the cashier's cubicle. She walked slowly over by the front desk, waiting to register after Thelma reappeared with her room key. Wearily, she rubbed the back of her neck as she watched the young women behind the counter smile and chat with the constant flow of hotel guests. It would be nice, she decided, to change into something cool like their flowered cotton shifts or the trim sports outfits worn by the women guests.

No wonder that Wayne Marshall hadn't wasted any time with her, she thought with wry amusement. By now, she felt as if she'd been up for thirty-six hours straight and probably looked it. It was a good thing that the Judge and Mrs. Byrne weren't there to see how quickly she'd been dropped by the only two eligible men she'd met! Scott Frazier hadn't even bothered with surface amenities and Wayne Marshall's courteous deference made her think that she'd better see about a new shade of lipstick as soon as she got back to the mainland. In the meantime, it was provident that she'd brought some books to read.

"These are for you." Thelma reappeared by her side and slipped two fragrant leis over her head. As Janet gave a gasp of surprise, the older woman smiled gently and added, "I should have said . . . *Aloha, Ianeke* . . . Welcome to Kaiulani."

Janet was charmed by the lilting liquid syllables. "And what should I answer?"

"*Mahalo* or *mahalo nui loa*. But that's enough for your first lesson. Now, come along with me. Your room's just past the main building in the new wing."

## THE CAPTURED HEART

Janet obediently followed her for a few steps and then pulled up. "But I forgot to register. Shouldn't I do that now?"

"It's all taken care of." Thelma held up a key. "I have your duplicate key in case we need it." She led the way down a flight of steps from the lobby to a center courtyard filled with palms and tropical foliage interspersed by a shallow, curving stream. The water was spanned at intervals by small half-moon Oriental bridges and bright orange carp moved lazily under them. Tiers of guest rooms rose above the courtyard with each balcony railing decorated by teak planter boxes and more greenery.

Janet was so busy trying to admire the surroundings that she had trouble keeping up with Thelma on the stone walkway beside the stream. She saw Bird's Nest Fern next to the fringe of Chinese Anthurium framing a carp pool which was dominated by a towering Fishtail palm. Next came a Pummelo tree with its smooth bark and grapefruit-like crop. Its roots, in turn, were covered by a creeper plant with purple flowers which provided cover for a flock of tiny brown birds to dart in and out of its sheltering leaves.

"This is the most beautiful place," breathed Janet in a hushed voice as Thelma waited for her to catch up. "I don't see how you ever get any work done."

"That's why we need a few people like Wayne to keep us going," the older woman said as they went down another flight of stairs and started down the long stone corridor of the guest wing. "Although some of us have been here so long that we forget and take it all for granted." Her expression was hard to read. "I've been here since the hotel was opened. I had to work, you see. Rodney's father was a fisherman and he was lost in a storm some years ago. The people here at Kaiulani have been good to me . . ." Her lips tightened for an instant and she frowned as they passed a petite Oriental maid wheeling a linen cart. The girl dropped her eyes and hurried past them without saying anything.

Janet started to comment and then changed her mind. Probably the girl was behind on her schedule and didn't want Thelma to know it. She glanced sideways at the older woman who nodded as if to confirm it.

"The help you get these days! *Auwe!* She knows the housekeeper's a good friend of mine."

"There seems to be so much staff here," Janet murmured, feeling a little sorry for the poor maid and wanting to change the subject.

"That's why Kaiulani is one of the famous hotels in the world," the other said. "We have one employee for every two guests."

"Good lord, I can't see how you keep them straight. There must be a terrific turnover."

"Not really." Thelma's tone was offhand. "You might enjoy seeing behind the scenes later on. I usually organize an official tour once a week but naturally I'd be glad to give you a private one." She smiled hesitantly. "If you're really interested."

## THE CAPTURED HEART

"Oh, I am. Of course, I have to give the Exhibit first priority—" She broke off as Thelma drew up before a guest room door and handed her the key. "Is this my room? I suppose my bags will be along . . ."

"Any minute now." Janet's hesitation seemed to puzzle the Hawaiian woman. "Is something wrong?" she asked.

"Well, no . . ." If Thelma wasn't going to show her into the room, there was certainly no reason to linger on the threshold, Janet decided. Evidently it wasn't part of the social director's regular duties. "I'm sure everything will be very comfortable," she assured the older woman. "Even if it isn't, I won't complain. Wayne told me how crowded the hotel is this week." She inserted her key in the lock and reached for the doorknob. "Thank you for bringing me down . . . I imagine I'll see you again tomorrow."

"Of course. I hope you'll enjoy every minute of your stay with us." Thelma seemed to be waiting for her to open the door, but as Janet lingered, she nodded reluctantly and started back up the corridor. She hadn't taken more than a step or two before she stopped abruptly and caught Janet halfway across the threshold. "Oh, I wanted to tell you that we'll send down some extra copies of the paper. You'd probably like to mail some to your friends."

Janet was still trying to make sense out of that when the door was abruptly pulled inward and she felt a firm masculine arm go around her shoulders.

"That would be very nice, Mrs. Kahori," Scott Fra-

33

zier told the now-beaming hostess. At the same time he exerted a warning pressure on Janet's upper arm when he saw her astonished expression change to outrage. He bent his head quickly as she opened her lips to protest. "Honey, I thought you'd never get here," he murmured fondly and then silenced her with such a firm and possessive kiss that every coherent thought left her head and she could only cling helplessly to the front of his shirt. Dimly she heard Thelma's chuckle and the the sound of her footsteps retreating on the stone floor.

As if that had been a signal, Scott raised his head and unceremoniously bundled Janet into the room, closing the door firmly behind them. Still keeping his hands on her shoulders, he cocked his head to listen. "I think that's convinced her," he said finally with some satisfaction and only then bothered to look down at Janet's flushed face. He must have sensed that she would have staggered if he'd released her because a whimsical expression passed over his stern features as he led her to the edge of a twin bed and made her sit down. "You look," he drawled calmly, "as if somebody had dropped a coconut on you. Maybe you'd better put your feet up."

By then, the effects of that kiss had worn off enough for Janet to realize that lying down and putting her feet up wasn't advisable under the circumstances. And that if anybody should be making suggestions, it wasn't the man who had phlegmatically settled on a wicker settee and put his own feet up on the coffee ta-

## THE CAPTURED HEART

ble across from her. Not only that, but he looked, she decided with developing outrage, as if he had every right to be there, and *she* was the interloper.

She stood up abruptly and glowered at him. "You have a hell of a nerve, I must say! I'll give you five seconds to get out that door before I call the manager or start screaming."

Scott merely leaned back against the chartreuse cushion on the settee. "That's what I like to hear. Now you're beginning to live up to that hair of yours. From what I saw on the pier, I didn't think you had it in you."

Janet's eyebrows drew together in an ominous line. "One . . ." she counted warningly, "two . . . three . . ."

"Come off it, honey. You haven't even got a decent case. But if it makes you feel better"—he jerked a thumb toward the table between the beds—"the telephone is right there."

Janet started toward it, but there was an undercurrent to his words that made her stop and stare at him over her shoulder. "What do you mean . . . I haven't a case? Since when has a simple letter of introduction given a man *carte blanche* to share a hotel room!"

"Since about an hour and a half ago. Save your adrenalin and take a look at the afternoon paper."

Her lips came together angrily. "What's all this about an afternoon paper? Wayne Marshall was talking about it and so was Mrs. Kahori."

"I'm not surprised." For the first time, Scott's tone was as annoyed as her own. He heaved himself erect

35

and went over to the desk at the end of the room and picked up the newspaper lying atop it. After handing it to Janet, he went back and sat down again.

"I don't see anything here," she said, scanning the headlines.

"Be thankful for small favors that it's not on the front page. Just keep going until the second section."

Obediently she thumbed through the pages as he ordered and then stopped, stricken by the sight of her likeness in a two-column picture flanked by a smaller one of Scott. Her glance skimmed a headline that announced "New Arrivals to Combine Business and Pleasure During Island Stay" and then moved down to the article below. "Scott and Janet Frazier," she read, "arrived at the luxurious resort of Kaiulani on Hawaii's northern coast today after flying in from the eastern mainland. They are in the enviable position of being able to combine business and pleasure during their trip to the big island. Mr. Frazier, a prominent corporate attorney in Manhattan, will confer with rancher clients during his stay on Hawaii, while his wife, Janet, will serve as an advance liaison director for the famed Oriental Art Exhibit opening at Kaiulani this weekend." Her jaw dropped as the words sank in. "Oh, no!"

"My reaction was remarkably similar," Scott said conversationally.

Janet turned on him fiercely. "How can you just sit there! Why didn't you say something, for heaven's sake. We can't let this farce go on."

## THE CAPTURED HEART

He held up a hand as she moved toward the telephone. "Nuh-uh . . . not so fast. Give me some credit . . . I reacted like that, too, but it isn't quite that simple. Now we have to find out how far this paper circulates. I can tell you this, though—for the time being we're committed to sharing the same nest for the weekend. Fortunately, it's a good-sized nest . . . there's a dressing room on the other side of the bath, so there's no need for complications."

"But that's ridiculous . . . all we have to do is ask for another room."

He shook his head. "Two people were turned down when I was registering and the woman at the desk was wondering how they were going to honor even their confirmed reservations. Your art exhibit has people coming out of the woodwork."

Janet remembered Rodney's comment which ran along the same lines. "Then you simply find another hotel," she said flatly.

"How many hotels did *you* see on the way up from Kona?"

"Well, none . . . but surely . . ."

"And how long a trip was it?"

"Over an hour," she admitted unwillingly.

"Exactly. My clients expect me to stay here. It was arranged a month ago." He smiled gently. "They also read the paper. Of course, *you* could find another hotel . . ."

"Don't be absurd . . . the art exhibit is going to be

held here. Everybody would think I was out of my mind."

"So we're back where we started . . . in communal if not conjugal bliss. We can work out the ground rules later. Right now"—he got up and stretched as she stared—"I'm going to take a shower. I was afraid it would give you too much of a shock if you found me there when you arrived."

"That was kind of you," she said sarcastically, not deigning to mention that his kiss didn't rate exactly as therapy. "Really, Mr. Frazier, you can't seriously think——"

"But I do." His voice cut through her expostulations like a whip. "I told you—I've gone over all the possibilities."

"Well, I haven't."

"Then we'll run through them again. *After* I've showered and after I've changed clothes. I'm sorry we have to share a bathroom but . . ."

"That's not the problem."

"Good! Then I'm not putting you out." He headed for a door at the end of the room, unbuttoning his shirt as he went.

She watched him, frowning. "Look here, Mr. Frazier . . ."

He turned wearily. "How about giving up on that 'Mr. Frazier' routine. The name's Scott." Her frozen expression prompted him to add, "You don't have to look so stricken about the way things have turned

# THE CAPTURED HEART

out. In this case, temporarily wedded does *not* mean bedded, honey."

"Well, I should hope not!" she exploded, clutching the newspaper in a death grip. "And stop calling me honey!"

Scott wasn't fazed by her outburst. He stood in the bathroom doorway and continued peeling off his shirt, revealing an expanse of tanned chest. "Well, I didn't think you were keen on Mrs. Frazier," he told her frankly, "and I've forgotten your first name. What was it . . . Jean . . . Joan?"

"Janet," she snapped, never believing a man could be so loathsome.

"Okay, then . . . Janet it is." He nodded absently and started to close the door, pausing just long enough to add, "You might call room service for coffee. We could use some when we try to figure out our next move. After that newspaper publicity, it'll have to be good."

Janet couldn't find anything wrong with that reasoning. Her expression lightened as she nodded and asked, "When do you want it? The coffee, I mean."

He glanced at his watch. "Fifteen minutes?"

"All right. I'll call right away."

"That's the girl—thanks, honey," he added absently and closed the bathroom door.

## Chapter Two

Janet stared at the closed bathroom door in utter frustration. For a second she was tempted to pound on it and let Scott Frazier know in no uncertain fashion that she wasn't used to being treated that way. Then the sound of the shower being turned on full force made her abandon the idea and go instead to the telephone. Scott wasn't the only one who needed coffee at this point. She sat down on the edge of the bed and wished heartily that she could collapse on it at full length. Instead, she put in the order to room service and then stood up again to inspect her surroundings.

The bedroom was furnished in a blending of teak and Italian wicker with color accents of tangerine and chartreuse on the Thai cotton bedspreads and upholstered furniture. The louvred panels and sliding

## THE CAPTURED HEART

screens at the far end of the room opened easily to reveal a spacious tiled lanai beyond. Janet pushed aside a screen panel to walk out in the brilliant sunshine and inspect a privacy planting of tropical bushes. Peering past the railing, she saw an expanse of lawn and then the inviting beach beyond. A line of graceful coconut palms rimmed the white sand to provide the final tropical touch. Far to the south, the looming mountain range showed its usual cloud cover but at Kaiulani the Hawaiian sun cloaked everything in ts cheerful rays.

Idly, Janet surveyed the two wicker chairs and a matching chaise lounge and experimentally dropped down on the latter to test its comfort. She frowned absently, wishing the hotel management had bestowed a little more padding on the porch furnishings. Obviously guests didn't spend much time on their lanais . . . even the sandy beach must feel softer.

After taking a deep breath of the fragrant air, she wandered back inside the room, making sure to close the screened panel behind her. She fingered a waxy anthurium flower in the stylized bouquet placed on the combination dressing table and counter before sitting down in one of the wicker chairs. As the water of the shower was turned off behind the closed door at the other end of the room, she acknowledged wryly that she had been aware of Scott's presence all the while. Restlessly she stood up to prowl the room again, hardly able to believe even then that this wasn't a figment of her imagination. And when it came to the prospect of sharing the same hotel suite, her tired mind bogged down completely. Surely there was some acceptable way to deny Wayne Marshall's story that would allow them to save face.

A calm, logical approach was all they needed, she told herself. Once Scott had cooled off with a shower and refreshed himself with a cup of coffee, he'd be amenable to her decision.

Her eyes narrowed as she saw her reflection in the mirror and she turned to search in her purse for her makeup kit. Just because her bags hadn't arrived and Scott had first priority with the shower didn't mean that she had to look like something left over from Hallowe'en.

A knock came on the hall door as she finished dusting some powder on her nose. She replaced her compact in her purse and went over to open the door as a second knock sounded. Outside, a porter was waiting patiently with her bags and a smiling waitress in an orange tutu-muu was carrying a tray of coffee things.

"Come in, please . . . both of you," Janet said.

The waitress nodded and headed directly toward the counter under the mirror with her tray but the porter paused and looked around inquiringly after putting the bags down by the nearest bed.

"There should be luggage racks," he murmured before starting purposefully toward the bathroom door. "Sometimes we store them in the linen closet."

Janet sidled hastily in front of him. "Don't bother. The bags are fine right there."

## THE CAPTURED HEART

The young porter pulled up abruptly. It was either that or push a hotel guest aside by brute force. He tried to explain. "It's no trouble, ma'am. We always keep luggage racks in each suite. If you'd rather, I can take the bags into the dressing room."

Janet's cheeks paled even more. "Oh, no . . . no, thank you. I'll take care of them myself later on." She was torn between the need to reach her purse on the coffee table for tip money and her reluctance to desert the bathroom door. All the time she was aware that the silence beyond the door was profound; evidently Scott could hear the conversation and was keeping discreetly quiet under the circumstances.

Janet managed to solve her dilemma. Urging the porter back toward the middle of the bedroom, she kept a flanking position on him as she reached for her wallet. She had bestowed his tip and was starting to sign the restaurant slip when the waitress gave a cluck of disgust.

"What's the matter?" Janet asked, keeping a wary glance on the porter, who was still eyeing the closed door. Clearly, the young man wasn't accustomed to leaving bags in the middle of the carpet and was ready to argue.

"Your cream," the waitress murmured. "I forgot the cream. You do like cream?" she asked, patently hoping for a denial.

Janet sighed. "Yes, please. I'd like cream." There was no point in lying politely. At that point, she needed all the caffeine in that coffee pot. "If you don't mind..."

The waitress nodded resignedly. "It will take only a few minutes. I'll be back, ma'am."

"No hurry." Janet managed to shepherd both of them out into the hall again.

"You should really move those bags, ma'am," the porter said, hanging in there.

"I'll take care of them right away," Janet smiled dismissingly as she closed the door. No sooner had the latch clicked and she'd leaned back against the cool wood than the bathroom door opened and Scott's toweled head appeared.

"Are they gone?" he asked.

She nodded. "You can come in now."

"Thanks a lot."

The irony of his tone wasn't lost on her. "Well, I'd just as soon not advertise this ridiculous situation," she said, bridling.

"Have it your way, but probably that same porter carried my bags here, so I don't know what you're proving." He headed for the far corner of the bedroom clad in a white terry-cloth robe and a pair of loafers. Halfway across he must have caught sight of her dismayed expression, because he explained: "Sorry about the informality but my shirts are in my other bag. I guess I left it in here." As she continued to stand beside the bed, he added irritably, "Look, have you anything against pouring that coffee?"

"No, of course not." She moved reluctantly over to

the tray. "I thought you'd want to wait until you're dressed."

"That won't take long." He toweled his thick hair absently with one hand before opening his suitcase on the nearest bed.

Just as if he had a right to half the bedroom, Janet decided with annoyance, as she noted his reflection in the mirror. Unfortunately, she was so intent on watching Scott's figure that she forgot to look at the stream of coffee she was pouring from an insulated carafe. "Ouch!" she exploded suddenly when the hot liquid cascaded onto her thumb and forefinger.

Scott's head jerked up. "What's the matter?"

"Oh, damn!" she drew the word out in pain and frustration as she waved her stinging hand in the air. "How could I be so stupid!"

Scott moved quickly to pluck the coffee pot from her other hand and put it back down on the tray before turning her toward the bathroom. "Go on in there and run cold water on the burn while I find some ointment in my first aid kit. Get going!" he ordered brusquely as she stood staring at him with wide eyes.

"I don't need anything . . ." she started to protest and then subsided quickly as her fingers throbbed. "All right, I'll go."

"That's the girl," he said, shoving her firmly toward the door. "It shouldn't take me long to find that tube of salve."

Janet had just disappeared into the bathroom and

turned on the water in the basin when the doorbell rang again.

"Oh, hell—now what?" Scott stopped in the middle of unzipping a leather toiletries kit to stride to the door.

The waitress held up a silver pitcher as he opened it. "I have your cream . . ." Her questioning glance went past him as she surveyed the room. "Mrs. Frazier . . . she asked for cream . . ."

"Thanks, I'll take it." He started to reach for some change in his pocket and then realized that he was still in his robe. "Wait just a second . . ."

"That's all right, sir." She beamed at him. "Mrs. Frazier took care of it earlier." She glanced across at the tray. "Is everything all right now?"

"Fine, thanks. It was nice of you to make a second trip." Scott gave her a perfunctory smile and started to close the door.

"Hey! Wait a minute, Frazier . . . you're just the man I want to see." Wayne Marshall came into view clutching an armful of newspapers. He nodded a pleasant dismissal to the waitress as he pulled up beside the door and shoved the newsprint at Scott. "I told your wife that I would get you some extra copies of the article. Thought you would like to have them to send to your family. Will four be enough," he peered into the bedroom beyond Scott's shoulders, "or do you want to ask Janet?"

"Four will be more than enough." Scott couldn't have been more definite.

# THE CAPTURED HEART

"You can never tell about women," Wayne said. "Maybe you'd better ask her and make sure."

Scott shrugged and walked back in the room to knock on the bathroom door.

It opened abruptly. "I thought you were going to get me that tube of first aid cream," Janet said, surveying his empty hands. "Couldn't you find it in your suitcase? Never mind—the cold water is helping."

"We have company," Scott cut in warningly. "Wayne Marshall is here," he jerked his head toward the corridor, "wondering how many copies you want of the story."

By then, the public relations man had come a discreet distance into the room and spoke over Scott's shoulder. "I couldn't help overhearing about the first aid cream. Is there anything I can do?"

"God forbid," Scott muttered. "You've done enough."

Wayne edged forward. "I beg your pardon . . ."

Janet squelched Scott with a look before grabbing a towel to wipe her dripping fingers. She came out into the bedroom saying, "Scott meant that you've done more than enough for us already. I just spilled some coffee on my hand . . . nothing serious." She waggled her fingers for evidence.

"Well, if you're sure . . ."

"Oh, I am." Janet was disconcertingly aware that Wayne accepted Scott's robed presence in the room as completely normal. Even now, it was almost too late to start explaining how he'd been misled by their

47

shared surname. She stalled a little longer. "It was kind of you to bring the extra copies of the paper. Wasn't it, Scott?"

"Sure thing. Just great!"

If Wayne noticed the marked lack of enthusiasm in Scott's comment, he didn't let on. "No trouble at all," he said, beaming at them impartially. "I've already had my secretary airmail a copy to Judge Byrne so he'll realize how much space our papers are giving anything connected with the Exhibit's opening." As Janet groped her way to the bed, he gave her a worried look. "You're sure you're okay? Maybe that burn is worse than you think."

For a minute, she couldn't even remember what he was talking about. She could only send a desperate SOS toward Scott who was leaning against a wicker chair.

"I'll get that first aid cream," he offered laconically and moved over to his suitcase. "Some rest wouldn't hurt you after I treat the burn."

"Good idea," Wayne concurred. "Remember, the hotel has a nurse and doctor within call if her hand needs more attention."

"Very kind of you," Scott murmured, unearthing the salve and hitching the belt on his robe tighter when he straightened. "This stuff drips. I'd better put it on over the basin in the bathroom," he told Janet.

"I can manage . . ."

"Don't be silly." He came round the bed and motioned her ahead of him. "If you'll excuse us, Marshall . . ."

"Of course." Wayne poked his head around the open doorway. "I'll probably see you both at the luau tonight."

"I didn't know there was one . . ." Janet began.

"There wasn't time to tell you," Scott said briefly as he uncapped the salve. "Turn your palm over . . ." He glanced up again. "Thanks for bringing the papers, Marshall. We'll talk to you later."

"Sure thing." The publicity man had just started to turn when the phone rang. "You're busy . . . I'll get it for you," he told them and moved over between the beds.

A premonition of unease reached Janet and Scott simultaneously.

"It isn't important," she called over her shoulder, unable to move from the basin as burn salve dripped down her fingers.

"Don't bother," Scott added, thrusting the tube into Janet's uninjured hand and looking around for something to clean the cream from his own fingers.

Wayne ignored them cheerfully and picked up the receiver. "The Fraziers's room," he announced. "Mr. Frazier? Yes, he's here. Can you hold the wire a minute, please . . . right now he's busy helping his wife. Hello . . . hello . . . are you still there? Okay—I thought we'd lost the connection. Mr. Frazier will be here in just a minute . . ." He turned and waved the receiver toward Scott as he shot out of the bathroom, still drying his hands. "Long distance for you," Wayne said. "I'll be going. See you both later," he added to Janet as he passed her on the way out.

She saw the door close behind him and went out into the bedroom as Scott picked up the receiver.

"Frazier," he announced tersely and then grimaced as he identified the voice at the other end of the long-distance wire. "Yes, sir . . . I came up this afternoon." He sank slowly onto the edge of the bed. "No . . . you didn't misunderstand the man . . . she's with me, as well."

Janet's small moan brought his gaze over to her. He stared dispassionately as he said, "I hadn't realized the news would spread quite so fast. From the Honolulu paper, eh? I gather that their legal department called you." His fingers tightened on the receiver. "No, Janet's from New York, too. As a matter of fact, she's the one in your letter. Well . . . actually, we'd met before . . . a couple of years ago. That won't be necessary—I'm sure Judge Byrne knows by now. The public relations man here at Kaiulani hasn't missed a trick. No, I'm not annoyed . . ." A surge of red crossed his cheekbones as he watched Janet cross her fingers. "We just would have preferred a little less publicity. Yes, sir, I'm planning to attend the ranchers' meeting later this week. After that, I'll be on my way home." He broke off at a spate of conversation from the other end of the wire. "That isn't necessary. We'd planned to fit in a honeymoon later on. Well, it's very kind of you," he added in a tone which meant nothing of the sort. "Yes, sir, I'll give her your best. Right. I'll be in touch in a day or so. Thanks for calling." Scott dropped the receiver onto the phone rest and rubbed his neck. "Damn it all to hell!"

"Your boss, I gather?"

"Who else?" Scott went over to pour some hot coffee. "He sent his congratulations and is even making sure the news gets in the Manhattan papers. By tomorrow, I imagine the drums will be announcing it along the Congo. My God, I could throttle Marshall."

"It's a little late for that."

"That's an understated cliché if I ever heard one." He took a swallow of coffee and then put the cup back on the saucer before going to his suitcase and pulling out a clean shirt. "There's only one thing left to do."

Janet surveyed him warily. "What do you mean?"

"We have to make it legal. Do you mind . . . getting out of the way, I mean." He paused in front of her and then moved her out of the bathroom doorway by lifting her aside.

"I didn't think you were asking how I felt about marrying you," she countered sarcastically, remaining stubbornly on the threshold. "The divine right of kings was tossed out of court a century ago, Mr. Frazier."

"Look, lady," he stood in the middle of the bathroom, unbuttoning his clean shirt, "you'll notice that I'm not out turning handsprings on the lawn. It was one thing when we simply had to arrange things for the weekend. Unfortunately, it's gotten out of hand." He went into the dressing room and came back, carrying a pair of slacks.

Janet stubbornly stayed where she was although her cheeks took on heightened color. "I don't see why we can't get through a few days and then just say later on that we've applied for an annulment."

"You must be out of your mind. We're both a little long in the tooth for something like that," he said scornfully. "Things are bad enough without looking like damned fools on a nonconsummation of marriage charge."

"There's no need to spell things out," she countered weakly.

"You're either in a state of shock or not using the brains you were born with. Perhaps you've forgotten that I work for a firm of attorneys," he pointed out in a silky tone. "Judge Byrne will have a few things to ask you, too. Now that we've gotten through that, would you mind closing the door behind you so I can put my pants on? Unless, of course, you've lost your squeamishness about such trivialities. It doesn't matter to me." His hands started to loosen the belt on his robe.

Janet slammed the door so hard that it vibrated on the hinges behind her. By the time Scott emerged fully dressed in a light gray suit a few minutes later, she was over by the lanai screen staring sightlessly through the louvres.

# THE CAPTURED HEART

Scott saw her rigid back and halted uncertainly by the foot of the nearest bed. "Look, honey, I'm sorry." His words came out with difficulty. "I shouldn't have taken my foul temper out on you. I know you're not any happier about this mix-up than I am."

Janet turned slowly to face him, her eyes bright with unshed tears. "I shouldn't have snapped at you, either," she admitted, finding it hard to quarrel any longer with the tall, well-dressed man who confronted her. "You're right about making it legal . . . I couldn't stand any more hanky-panky about this. What should we do?"

"Make things an accomplished fact as soon as possible." He spoke quietly but firmly. "There's an airport at Waimea which isn't too far from here. I'll phone a friend of mine in the courthouse at Hilo and tell him I'm on my way for the license." He moved over to the desk and opened his briefcase. Extracting a paper from one side of it, he said, "Come over and sign this. Then put down all your vital statistics on that piece of notepaper . . ."

She moved over beside him and took the pen he was holding toward her. "All right. What vital statistics do you mean?"

"Age . . . birthplace . . . middle name . . . parents' names. You know the kind of stuff on a marriage license application."

Her chin went up. "No, I don't. This is the first time I've ever done anything like this."

"I'm not intimately acquainted with it myself," he

countered, "but I have a good imagination. Pretend you're applying for a civil service job."

"Or death benefits," she said sweetly, bent over the desk.

"Exactly. Don't worry if you forget something. I can fill it in later."

"Thanks, but I don't think it will be necessary." She gave him the piece of paper and watched him scan it hastily before shoving it in his coat pocket. "I gather that I don't have to go along?"

"There's no point. I want to pick up the license without causing any more comment than necessary. Tomorrow we can visit a minister I know on the northern end of the island. After the ceremony, nobody will pay any attention to the date on the license, so there shouldn't be any publicity. That's one advantage to being eight thousand miles away from home."

"It's about time we got the breaks on something," Janet told him with some bitterness. "What should I do while you're gone?"

Scott paused with his hand on the doorknob, a trifle disconcerted. "I don't know. Why?"

"Well, what should I say if anybody asks where you are?"

"Just look vague and tell them I'm working." He pulled open the door. "I'll come along to the luau if I'm not too late getting a flight back."

Janet started to say that it would be better if he spent the night in Hilo but paused when he gave her a sardonic look over his shoulder.

"Togetherness is the watchword, honey," he said. "You'd better get used to it," and was gone up the corridor before she could reply.

## Chapter Three

Later that evening when it was time to dress for the luau, Janet had become partially reconciled to her changed status in life. She didn't know whether her newfound peace of mind came from the fact that Scott had left the hotel or whether it was the result of asking the Kaiulani switchboard not to put through any more long-distance calls. She had decided that Scott's physical presence played enough havoc with her pulse rate—without having to explain her sudden matrimonial plunge to the Byrnes as well.

She hung her clothes in one of the large closets in the dressing room and then, after spending a restless half hour atop the lounge on the lanai, decided on a leisurely bath before dressing for the luau.

The Kaiulani management had thoughtfully provided a packet of herbal bubble bath, and Janet hap-

# THE CAPTURED HEART

pily relaxed in the frothy, sweet-smelling water. It took sheer willpower to eventually get out of the tub and use the immense terry bath sheet with the hotel's distinctive hibiscus trim. She had just finished dressing in a pair of green shantung evening pajamas with a cowl-neck overblouse when she heard a timid knock and the sound of a key being inserted in the door on the corridor. Warily she poked her head around the bathroom door to see the tiny Oriental maid enter with a pile of clean towels over her arm.

The girl paused, startled, when she saw Janet's figure.

"It's all right . . . go ahead with your work," Janet told her as the maid took a hesitant step backward. "Have you come to change the towels?" She paused as the girl with her glossy bobbed hair stared uncomprehendingly at her. "Do you speak English?" Janet asked slowly and distinctly, only to rouse a small but negative response. The maid shook her head. "Well, it doesn't matter." Janet smiled and decided to try charades. First, she pointed to the towels and waved toward the bath. Then, she pantomimed turning back the spread on the bed.

The worried look on the maid's face was replaced with a shy smile before she scurried obediently into the bathroom. It didn't take her long to change the towels and afterward return to the bedroom to fold the bedspreads neatly and whisk them onto the top shelf of the closet. A carafe of ice water was brought from her cart and put on the table between the beds.

Then two plumeria blossoms were deposited on each pillow. The maid's dark-eyed glance went around the room in a final survey before she bobbed her head shyly in farewell and closed the door behind her.

Janet walked slowly over to pick up one of the blooms from the pillowcase. The plumeria's pungent perfume reminded her of the leis which Thelma Kahori had given her earlier. She dropped the flower back on the bed and went over to take the garlands from the tiny refrigerator in the corner bar. They would add just the right island touch to her outfit, she decided, admiring the ivory and orchid-colored blossoms against the green shantung.

She caught up her purse and room key, decided against the need for any evening wrap, and let herself out into the corridor.

Thelma Kahori, still in her dark muu-muu, met her as she emerged from a nearby service stair. "Good evening, Mrs. Frazier. Are you on your way to the luau?" She frowned slightly and glanced over Janet's shoulder. "Surely you're not alone. Isn't Mr. Frazier feeling well tonight?"

"He's fine, thanks," Janet said offhandedly, as if explaining away an absent husband happened all the time. "An unexpected business appointment cropped up and he may be a little late in getting back to the hotel."

"Rodney mentioned that he saw him driving away but I told him he must be mistaken. Mr. Frazier won't have any vacation at all at this rate. You'll have to put your foot down," she added in motherly fashion as she walked beside her.

Janet ignored the inviting prospects of any woman telling Scott Frazier what to do. "You don't have to worry about me," she told Thelma. "I'm used to being on my own."

"I didn't *think* you'd been married long." The hostess's eyes gleamed with fun. "I'll bet you're still on your honeymoon."

"No—you're wrong about that," Janet was able to say with perfect truthfulness.

"Well, practically newlyweds, then."

"You could say that." Janet deliberately switched subjects before Thelma could probe further. "The maid was just in checking the room. I thought the plumeria blossoms she left on the pillow were such a nice touch. It reminded me of the miniature chocolate bar with 'Bonne Nuit' on the label that they leave in European hotels . . . but this is even nicer."

"Most of our guests comment on it. I hope everything else was satisfactory." When the elevator door slid noiselessly open, Thelma motioned Janet in and then pushed the button for the lobby level.

"The maid and I didn't have much of a discussion. Does she speak any English?" Janet asked.

"Some of our girls come from the smaller villages around here. In the close-knit communities they still use a kind of 'pidgin' dialect," Thelma explained.

"I never thought of that." Janet frowned slightly as they stepped out into the lobby. "For a minute, I was sure I'd seen her before but now I'll never know."

"If it's important, I could ask the housekeeper. She's a friend of mine."

"Heavens, no!" As Thelma paused by the front desk, Janet added, "You'll have to give me directions on how to find the luau. Is it nearby?"

"Not far from here. Take those steps at the far end of the lobby. They lead down to a path which follows the sea wall to the Garden Pavilion. You can't miss seeing the torches and hearing the music."

"It sounds lovely," Janet smiled. "I'll be on my way."

"And don't worry . . . I'll tell Mr. Frazier where to find you if I see him."

"Mr. Frazier?" For an instant, Janet forgot her altered status. Then reality flooded back, "Oh, you mean Scott," she murmured to cover her lapse. "He may be very late, so I'll just expect him when I see him. Good night, Mrs. Kahori." She nodded and made her way to the steps Thelma had indicated, hoping that the social director wouldn't dwell on the missing bridegroom.

The remnants of a spectacular sunset still remained in the sky as she reached the bottom of the steps and followed a path along a sea wall constructed from native stone. Once the last streaks of orange disappeared from the horizon, darkness dropped like a cloak around her. The warmth of the day lingered longer and the faint whisper of a breeze was softly caressing on her shoulders. She leaned over the low wall to stare at the waves cascading rhythmically over the floodlit rocks below. As she stood there, a mammoth ray, attracted by the light, swam into the shallow water. The big fish hovered near the surface and then showed its mottled white belly as it circled past the rocks to head for the open sea again.

"So this is where you are!" Wayne Marshall, wearing a flowered Hawaiian shirt and light slacks, strolled up beside her. "There won't be any food left if you don't come along. The festivities started an hour ago."

Janet was reluctant to move. "Did you know there was the most tremendous fish down there just now . . . it was at least eight feet across."

Wayne grinned. "That's Charlie, our manta ray. He comes along most nights. We toss a little food in for him . . . makes a nice touch, if I do say so."

She felt an instant's letdown. "Oh, darn! I thought it was unusual."

"Well, it is. He's not under contract, you know. And Charlie's not discriminating in his diet so don't offer him any fingers or arms. He'd take them." Wayne looked around absently. "Where's that husband of yours?"

Janet's lips tightened. She hadn't realized that appearing without one's husband caused as much comment as a see-through blouse. "He plans to come along later," she replied, trying not to sound as annoyed as she felt. It was too bad she couldn't tell him that Scott wasn't under contract yet, either. "Is the luau on down this path?"

He fell into step beside her. "Just behind that big Kiawe tree."

"Oh, of course. I can hear the music now."

"You'll see all the lights in a minute," he promised. "There's such thick foliage along these paths that you have to know where you're going."

A little farther along and they turned into a brightly lit clearing filled with picnic tables and people. Most of the guests congregated at the pergola, which was being used as a makeshift bar, or at the long table sagging under a magnificent buffet. Beyond the end of it, four Hawaiian musicians played on a small spotlighted stage by the trunk of the Kiawe tree.

"The Bristows have been asking for you," Wayne said. "They're at a table over by the band. If you want to join them, I'll get you some food."

"All right, but you don't have to wait on me."

"I know I don't. Besides, I'm officially off-duty. This comes under the heading of a fringe benefit." He grinned at her ruefully. "Too bad you didn't visit Kaiulani sooner—before that husband of yours came into view."

Janet opened her mouth and then closed it again. It was long past the time for confessions and in her new status, even a minor flirtation wouldn't be allowed. She glanced across at Wayne's pleasant features and sighed. After Scott's high-handed assurance, the amiable publicity man appealed to her bruised ego.

"Janet . . . over here!"

She looked over to see Bonita Bristow in a wild orange muu-muu beckoning toward their table.

"Go ahead," Wayne said. "I'll collect something for us to eat and be right with you."

She nodded and threaded her way through the other tables before sliding onto the bench next to Bonita. "It's nice to see you again——" she began politely when Martin, clad in a matching orange shirt, interrupted her from across the table.

"We were going to call and have you join us for some drinks," he said abruptly. "But that man Marshall said probably your husband had other plans. I didn't know you had a husband stashed away out here," he added accusingly.

"I never thought to mention it," Janet replied quite truthfully. "How do you like the hotel by now?"

Bonita raised her eyebrows expressively. "I could get used to this kind of life," she said. "And wait till you try the food!" She gestured at the heaped monkeypod platter in front of her. "There are so many calories that it's almost indecent." She gestured as Wayne brought two more heaped platters to the table and sat down beside Martin. "See what I mean."

"I'll never be able to eat all that food," Janet protested.

"Well, I wasn't sure what you wanted so I took a

little of everything," Wayne reassured her. "If you don't want to go native, you can just eat the steak."

Janet surveyed the various compartments on her wooden dish. "Other than the steak, I don't recognize a thing. I need somebody to translate."

Wayne leaned across the table and pointed with his fork. "Okay. Clockwise, that's a portion of *low-low*, the next is——"

"Wait a minute . . . what's *low-low?*" she persisted.

"A mixture of cooked fish and pork wrapped in a ti leaf. The concoction next to it is our specialty of chicken and long rice. Under the hot sauce in the center you'll find shrimp and that's a wedge of fresh coconut on the edge of the platter."

She nodded. "I even recognize the baked banana next to it, but what's the mixture that looks like Cream of Wheat?"

"*Taro,*" Martin put in. "It's the islanders' staple. For my money, you can call it 'cooked nothing.'"

"Most of our guests like to try it once," Wayne explained smoothly. "After that, you're on your own."

"I'll have to admit that your food's damned good," Martin said. "And you spared us the pig on a spit with hot rocks inside. Every other luau's had one of those." He paused for a swallow from his glass of beer before asking Wayne, "Any chance of a preview on this art exhibit? I'd especially like to see that temple drum I've read about."

"So would a lot of other people," Wayne replied,

# THE CAPTURED HEART

"but the insurance companies are raising cain about our security. 'Fraid we can't make any exceptions unless Mrs. Frazier appoints you as her assistant. She'll be checking the exhibits early, I suppose."

"That's what I came to do," Janet said, amazed that she'd forgotten about her job ever since her arrival on the island. "But just in connection with the later showings on the mainland. I don't pull any weight here despite what Wayne says."

"I wondered when I read that article in the paper this afternoon," Martin said, finishing his food and gesturing for a waitress to remove the platter. "Well, I can wait. Kaiulani looks like a good place to loaf for a few days."

"Some time off will be good for you," his wife told him briskly. She tilted her blonde head for a minute to listen to the music and then put out a demanding hand. "You can start your therapy by dancing with me . . . that's our kind of music."

Martin stood up quickly, even as he shook his head in mock protest. "Henpecked already," he told Wayne before he shepherded Bonita onto the cleared space between the tables. "You can see why I need this vacation. Excuse us, please."

Wayne had risen to his feet, and instead of sitting back down, he held out a hand to Janet. "We'd better get our exercise now, too. Later on, they'll be teaching everybody to hula. That's to be avoided at all costs unless you like sore muscles."

After an instant's hesitation, Janet got up beside

him. On the dance floor, he pulled her firmly against him and grinned when she looked up in surprise. "An old Hawaiian custom," he said, lowering his cheek to hers.

They danced in silent harmony after that; a tribute to the soft, lilting melody, the warm, tropical night and the effortless ease with which their steps merged. When the music ended, Janet was astonished to see that they had threaded their way beyond the tables and were on a dimly lit platform by the sea wall.

She pushed back from Wayne's clasp and took a deep breath.

He grinned appreciatively. "Pretty heady atmosphere, isn't it? I'm beginning to understand why we attract so many honeymooners here." His expression sobered. "How long have you been married?"

"Long enough to know that I'd better get back and finish dinner." She reached up to smooth her hair. "The Bristows will be wondering what happened to us."

"To say nothing of your husband." The publicity man was watching her closely.

"Scott?" She gestured airily with one hand. "Scott has other things to think about."

It was obvious immediately that she'd made the wrong remark. Wayne's eyes widened slightly and then he moved to close the distance between them. "In that case, what are we waiting for?" he said, pulling her into his arms.

"Oh, no . . . please . . . I didn't mean . . ." Jan-

THE CAPTURED HEART

et's immediate protest was submerged by a more forceful one behind her.

"Mrs. Kahori said I'd find you at the luau," Scott announced in a cold, accusing voice. His glance flicked dismissingly over the other man. "Nice of you to look after her, Marshall. Now, if you'll excuse us . . ."

He had propelled her six feet down the path before Janet recovered from her surprise. "But the luau!" she squeaked. "Aren't you going to have anything to eat?"

"I ate earlier."

"Janet didn't have much," Marshall put in.

Scott's fingers tightened on her elbow. "Is that so?" He sounded patently disinterested. "Then I should have thought she'd be eating rather than dancing." Before Wayne could comment, he went on. "It doesn't matter. We can order something in our room. G'night, Marshall."

"*Must* you keep a hammerlock on me?" Janet gritted out between her teeth as he marched her down the darkened path in a silence as heavy as the moist air around them. She yanked her arm away. "At this rate, I'll be black and blue."

"You're damned lucky you aren't red in a certain area besides," he growled as he slowed his steps to stare down at her. "What in the hell do you mean by necking with that publicity ape the minute I turn my back?"

67

"Necking!" Her voice went up an octave. "Well, I *like* that——"

"So I noticed." Like an angry schoolmaster, he cut in before she could finish. "It's a good thing I got there when I did."

"Nothing happened, I tell you. All I did was dance with the man." Janet was so angry that she could hardly get the words out.

"Oh, sure." His deep tone was thick with sarcasm. "What was wrong with the dance floor? Everybody else was using it."

"There wasn't anything wrong with it—" Janet broke off as she realized that he might have a reason for annoyance. Instead of acknowledging it, however, she rashly kept on her course. "I can tell you right now, though, that I'm *not* accustomed to being treated like this. You might as well learn that I'll do *what* I please, *when* I please, and with *whom* I please."

"In a pig's eye, honey." Scott's eyes glinted. "The rules changed when you walked in this hotel, and while we're here, I'll see that you remember."

"You don't have any right—"

"After eleven o'clock tomorrow, I'll have plenty of them. That's when we see the minister at Mahukona." He nudged her on down the path. "It's all arranged."

His announcement made her forget her anger. "Then you got the license?"

He tapped his breast pocket. "Right here. I didn't think I should leave it in the room."

## THE CAPTURED HEART

She nodded. "I can see your point, although I don't think our maid knows any English."

"You saw her?"

"The maid?" Janet frowned as she glanced up at him. "Yes, she brought some towels before I went to dinner. Why?"

He ignored her question to ask his own. "And everything was all right then?"

"Of course." She pulled up again in the middle of the path. "What's happened?"

"I stopped by the room for a minute when I got back. Somebody had been searching the luggage. None of my stuff's missing and your watch was still on the desk, so it wasn't a sneak thief." He smiled slightly. "I presume that it wasn't your doing?"

"Hardly. I don't know where you got your ideas about women but you certainly have some strange ones."

"Well, that's a relief." His grin broadened. "At least I won't have to worry about hiding my wallet every night."

"For the short time we're going to be together, you're as safe as houses." She started walking again. "I don't like the idea of people snooping, though. Kaiulani's the last place in the world I would have expected it."

Scott rang for the elevator as they reached the beach wing of the hotel. "Was there anything worth ransacking in your stuff . . . other than the obvious?"

"I don't think so." She frowned as she tried to

think. "Right now, my mind's an utter blank."

"Don't worry about it. Once we get in the room, you'll remember." He motioned her ahead of him into the elevator. "That's the main reason I dragged you away from the luau in such a hurry."

"Oh." Janet was aware that her response was weak but she was still trying to align his explanation with her own reaction to what had happened. When Scott had confronted her and Wayne by the sea wall, she'd been aware of only one emotion from him; anger . . . pure and simple. Such seething anger that her pulse was still pounding as a result of it. Yet now he claimed that the room ransacking was the main reason for taking her from the luau. "What was the other one?" she wondered aloud.

"I beg your pardon?"

"Never mind." She decided not to pursue the subject as his expression turned impassive once again. "It wasn't important. Do you have your key handy?"

"Right here." He reached in his coat pocket and brought it out as they turned from the corridor and stopped in front of their door. Unlocking it, he gestured her in ahead of him and went over to lean against the wall as he watched her start a cursory search of her things. "No luck?" he asked finally as she straightened and sighed.

"I can't see a thing missing," she admitted.

"How about the art exhibit data?"

"That's in an attaché case somewhere." She

# THE CAPTURED HEART

frowned as she looked around the room. "There it is on the desk."

"Better take a look."

She shrugged and followed his suggestion, unzipping the case to leaf through a thin stack of papers. Then, more intently, she went through them one by one. "How did you guess?" she asked finally.

"There had to be something if they were ignoring jewelry and cash. What did they take?"

"A special list of display items."

He frowned and shifted his shoulders restlessly. "I don't get it. That information was published in the show catalogue, wasn't it?"

"Not exactly. They kept a few items out deliberately for security reasons. The choicest ones, Judge Byrne said. And there was one other thing about my list..."

Scott was rubbing his thumb along his jawbone but at her words he stopped. "What was that?"

"It had the insured value of the special exhibits on it."

He whistled softly. "Where do you go from here?"

"All I can do is telephone Judge Byrne tomorrow." She looked thoughtful. "And report it to Wayne Marshall, of course, since he's handling the arrangements here at Kaiulani."

"Wouldn't he have a duplicate list?"

Janet slowly shook her head. "Not with the valuations. The insurance people were chary about putting it down on paper." Her troubled expression robbed her of the last vestige of sophistication. Scott thought fleetingly that she looked like a woeful child.

"Don't take it so seriously." His voice softened perceptibly. "The sun will still come up tomorrow morning."

She gave him the ghost of a grin. "You don't have to explain to the Judge. How could I have been so careless?"

"We had a few other things on our minds." He straightened and shoved his hands in his pockets. "If you need a good defense lawyer, I'll volunteer my services. Now, you'd better get some sleep," he added matter-of-factly. "Tomorrow's going to be a busy day."

"I hadn't forgotten." She kept her tone as casual as his. "What do we do about tonight?"

"You don't waste time with diplomacy, do you? It must be that red hair of yours." He had bent down and was stacking the seat cushions from the wicker settee as he spoke.

She stayed by the edge of the desk. "Probably. What are you going to do with those?"

"I had an idea that you might be difficult ... about sharing the bedroom tonight, I mean."

"Don't bother to spell it out," she cut in coldly. "I'm happy I got the idea across."

"So I gathered." He picked up the cushions and headed for the bathroom door. "Bring along a pillow and a blanket, will you?"

Puzzled, she did as he asked and followed him

through the bathroom into the dressing room beyond, where he was dealing out the cushions in a line on the rug. "Put that stuff down anywhere. I'll get it later," he ordered, intent on his task.

She deposited the bedclothes on a bureau as if they were made of glass before saying, "I thought you'd go out on the lanai."

He looked up then. "There are aquariums with more privacy than that thing. Let's not cause any more comment than we have already."

"You don't have to lecture me. Knock on the door when you're finished with the bathroom." His raised eyebrows made her wonder for a second if she'd gone too far. "About tomorrow morning——"

"I'll be up," he said, cutting her off. "Good night, Janet."

For some reason she was tempted to linger, to prolong the discussion until she decided to terminate it. But while she was still hovering uncertainly by the door, Scott took off his coat, undid his tie and started to unbutton his shirt. Deliberately, she was sure.

"Good night," she muttered almost inaudibly. "Let me know if you want anything . . ." There was a pause as she realized she'd chosen the wrong words. She tried again, "I mean, if you need anything—just let me . . ." From the corner of her eye, she saw his broad chest start to shake with silent laughter. At that point, she flushed, gave up, and beat an ignominious retreat—slamming the bathroom door behind her.

## Chapter Four

"Rise and shine, honey."

The words were accompanied by a firm hand on Janet's shoulder. Both happenings were novel enough to make her stir restlessly on her pillow and then sit up in bed so suddenly that Scott, who was still bending over her, had to fend her off. "Hey, slow down. It's not *that* late."

She blinked at him as she clutched a handful of sheet to her breast. "What are you doing here?"

He sighed audibly. "I *live* here . . . remember."

"You're already dressed." Her accusing gaze moved past him to see the room restored to normal with settee cushions in place and the pillow back on the bed next to her. She started to frown as she belatedly noticed the rumpled sheets and blanket below it.

Scott cut in before she could say anything. "Relax

# THE CAPTURED HEART

. . . honey. Pure window-dressing. Your reputation's still pure and unsullied. I thought the bed looked better that way than untouched."

"Umm." She was acutely aware that his masculine gaze hadn't missed a detail of her mussed hair and undoubtedly shiny nose. "Would you please hand me my robe," she said stiffly.

He shook his head. "You won't need it. I'm off to breakfast right now. Room service is bringing your orange juice, coffee, and sweet rolls in fifteen minutes. If you'd rather have something else . . ."

"No, that's fine. Thanks. Usually I just have a piece of toast and coffee."

He stopped by the door to give her an appraising glance. "You could stand a few more pounds, but this isn't the time to worry about it. Can you be ready to go by the time I get back?"

"Why . . . yes."

"Good. I'll see you later."

When he had gone, Janet got up to survey her figure in the mirror. She smoothed her pajamas at the hipline, then wrinkled her nose at her reflection. A few more pounds indeed! The man didn't know the first thing about measurements and she'd certainly tell him so.

She turned and looked at the empty room bleakly, which was ridiculous, she told herself. Privacy was the very thing she craved. She'd make that clear to Scott before their charade went any further. Then the face of her travel clock reminded her that she'd have to hurry with her shower if she were to be dressed by the time her breakfast tray was delivered.

Afterwards, she had just zipped up a cool white dress embroidered with tiny tulips and realized that it was going to serve as her wedding dress when a knock came on the door to announce the arrival of her breakfast. Deliberately she relegated the thought of matrimony to the back of her mind. If she dwelt on it, she'd be too nervous to eat anything.

A few minutes later, another knock revealed the elfin figure of the hotel maid she'd seen the night before. This time, Janet didn't bother with words . . . she simply smiled, beckoned her in, and left her to it while she finished breakfast. When the telephone rang and Janet picked up the receiver, the Oriental girl abandoned her bedmaking and discreetly went in to change the towels.

"Hello," Janet said hesitantly, wondering if she were going to have to tell Judge Byrne about the theft of the exhibit list sooner than she'd planned. The announcement of her wedding would be enough to send the Byrnes reeling; the theft would add a knockout blow. Any more catastrophes and he'd tell her not to bother with a return ticket.

"Hello . . . Janet, is that you?" Scott's firm voice broke into her mental wanderings.

She took a deep breath. "Yes. I'm all ready."

"Good. I'll get the car and meet you out front. By the way," his tone lost a little of its assurance, "I met Wayne Marshall in the lobby a minute ago and men-

## THE CAPTURED HEART

tioned that our room was ransacked last night. When he asked if we were missing anything, I told him about the loss of that list."

"I'm glad you did," she admitted frankly. "I've been avoiding it ever since I got up. What's he going to do?"

"Phone the insurance company right away and report it to hotel security. The local police will undoubtedly contact the law enforcement people in Hilo. Wayne thinks there might be trouble when the stuff goes on display. It looks as if somebody's deciding the best thing to take."

"That's what I was afraid of."

"For pete's sake, don't go into a decline over it. Maybe the disappearance of that list will be a good thing in the long run. At least Kaiulani's doubling the security precautions."

"Then I don't have to see Wayne this morning?"

There was a slight pause. "Not unless you want to," Scott replied. "I told him we had some things planned." His voice became brusque again. "Five minutes? In the drive?"

"I'm on my way." As she replaced the receiver, Janet smiled faintly. Evidently Scott wasn't as blasé about the morning's activities as he'd have her believe. She picked up a white linen pouch bag and a small-brimmed hat of the same material. She surveyed the latter ruefully, thinking it was a far cry from the confections of blossoms and tulle usually associated with weddings. Of course, under the circumstances, it didn't matter. Her eyes suddenly swam with tears and she reached for a handkerchief to blow her nose with some annoyance. Thank goodness, there was no one to watch her behaving like an idiot.

A shuffling noise in the bathroom made her remember that she wasn't alone. The slight figure of the maid wrapped in her oversized uniform hovered in the doorway. She peered at Janet's unhappy face with an expression of understanding which showed that some things didn't need translating.

Janet tried to think of something to say, then shook her head and simply gave her a watery smile before she went out. She encountered Thelma Kahori in the corridor again on the way to the elevator.

"Good morning, Mrs. Frazier." Today the hostess was in a voluminous dark green muu-muu trimmed with a hemline ruffle. "Or should I say '*Aloha kakahiaka,*' to put you in the right mood?"

Her cheerful tones made Janet feel better immediately. "It's such a pretty day and this is such a beautiful place . . . you don't have to say a thing."

"We feel that way, too," the older woman said simply. Her glance went over Janet's outfit. "You look very elegant. It seems nice to see something other than casual clothes around here."

"We're going out for a drive and I'm not sure where we'll have lunch," Janet explained, trying to sound as if she dressed in heels and a hat for all her sightseeing expeditions. A typewritten list in Thelma's hand helped her to change the subject. "If

## THE CAPTURED HEART

you're looking for the maid, I left her in our room. She's almost finished, I think."

"Good. I wanted to catch her." Thelma started to move off and then paused again. "Her work's satisfactory today?"

"Oh, yes." Janet wavered as she remembered the missing list and then decided against mentioning it. "Perfectly satisfactory."

Thelma frowned as she noticed the hesitation. "What is it, Mrs. Frazier?"

Janet sought a plausible answer. "Nothing really. I was just going to say that I wished I could speak to her. Sign language has its limitations, but it doesn't matter." She checked her watch and grimaced. "I'll have to run . . . see you later." Rather than wait for the elevator, she hurried to the stairs and left the social director staring thoughtfully after her.

Scott had parked in the curving hotel drive and was standing beside the car waiting for her. She had only a minute to notice that he had put on an oyster-colored blazer over a crisp gray shirt and slacks for the occasion. The contrast between the neutral colors of his outfit and his tanned skin made her realize forcibly again what a good-looking man he was. This discovery succeeded in disconcerting her so that she was completely breathless when she reached his side.

"You didn't have to hurry that much," he commented, unaware of the reason for her confusion. "I've collected a lunch to take with us . . . for a picnic later, if that sounds good. Incidentally, you look very nice." The last was added almost awkwardly.

"So do you." The words were out before Janet realized it. In the resulting pause, she managed a tremulous smile and then slid onto the front seat.

Scott reached over her shoulder to take a fragrant lei from a plastic bag on the back seat. "I got this for you in Hilo yesterday," he said as she murmured with pleasure. "I'm glad it goes with your dress."

She buried her nose in the fragrant blossoms and took a deep breath. "The colors are lovely and would go with anything. I recognize the red ginger leaves and the plumeria . . . what are the tiny white ones?"

"Crown flowers, I think." He'd gotten behind the wheel and pulled out into the curving drive. His attention was on the road as they drove along the golf course, keeping a sharp lookout for electric golf carts. Once they reached the main road, he turned north and increased his speed.

"There's a small Anglican chapel up close to Mahukona at the end of the island," Scott informed her. "It's run by Father Lehua. He had a church on the mainland for years, but after he retired he wanted to come home to the big island. I met him a couple years ago."

"You don't think he'll have read the newspapers?"

Scott shook his head. "Not Father Lehua. All he cares about is his sermon for Sunday and whether the fish are biting off the coast."

"I wish we didn't have to feel so underhanded

about this," Janet said in a low voice. "You're sure everything will be legal?"

"And me a lawyer?" Scott shot her a sideways glance. "Don't worry. Father Lehua will even put it in his records . . . when he gets around to it. By then, nobody will remember or care if there's a small discrepancy in the dates." He smiled sardonically. "Compared to the jet set, we're lily-white. Most of them don't bother about such formalities."

Janet's cheeks took on a touch of color. "I don't do things that way."

"Believe it or not, that makes a nice change." His voice was dispassionate. "Once we tie the knot, we can set about extricating ourselves."

"In a safe, legal manner."

He must have heard the acid in her tone, because he managed to give her a quick look as he stopped at an intersection before turning onto a narrow road which skirted the mountains.

"That's what you wanted, isn't it?" he asked. "I thought we'd agreed on that."

"I wasn't arguing about it," she said stiffly, unable to admit that his discussion of a divorce before they were even married was scarcely flattering to a woman's ego. "How much farther to this Mahukona?"

"About forty-five minutes. It's through ranch country most of the way." He nodded to the lush green grassland which rose sharply from the road on either side. A few Black Angus cattle were grazing in pastures bounded by barbed wire and fence posts made of gnarled wood. At intervals, signs saying "Kapu" or "No Trespassing" warned intruders away. A flock of tiny gray birds fluttered into flight as the car approached and then quickly settled back to their fence-sitting again. Far down to the left, beyond a landscape dotted with fern-leaved Kiawe trees, Janet was able to see the still gray-blue of the Pacific. She smiled as they passed another small herd of cattle who stared at the car as it passed.

"What's the joke?" Scott asked, noting her amusement.

"All that lovely view," she explained, "and the cows just turn their backs on it. A real estate broker would go mad if he saw it."

"Don't think that developers haven't thought of it. But the ranchers around here like it just the way it is . . . unspoiled, peaceful . . ."

"And incredibly beautiful," she finished for him.

From then on, the drive passed in a restful silence as they enjoyed the deserted country road which wound and dipped around the Kohala Mountains. Finally, at an unmarked intersection, Scott turned toward the sea and they descended from the mountain pastures back into the vestiges of civilization. At first, there were small land-holdings of a few acres with simple, metal-roofed houses. Then, city lots side by side until a signpost of King Kamehameha indicated they were in the town of Mahukona itself.

Scott made another turn to the left as they reached

the main street. "The church is down here a little way. It won't be long now."

"Are we on time?"

"Close enough." He grinned. "Father Lehua said he'd postpone his nap if we weren't."

Janet felt a moment of panic. "What about witnesses?"

"Relax, honey. He promised to furnish them."

"I wish you'd stop calling me honey," Janet protested, relieved that she could find a legitimate complaint. When he simply grinned more broadly, she gave up and used the mirror on the back of the sun visor to adjust her hat.

Scott slowed at the outskirts of the village to allow Janet her first glimpse of St. Andrews Near the Sea. It was a small white clapboard church that looked as if it should have been decorating the Vermont countryside rather than a tropical island. The slender spire might have been transplanted from New England, but it stood proudly in the midst of some tall Cook Pines. An old burial ground occupied the land at the front of the church, and a narrow flagstone walk wound its way past the monuments to the front steps.

As Scott parked the car nearby, she caught a glimpse of the carved entrance doors being opened, and when they made their way up the walk a few minutes later, an elderly man in white vestments stood waiting in the arch to greet them.

"Janet . . . this is Father Lehua," Scott said simply as they stopped beside him.

"Welcome to St. Andrews, my dear." The priest's white hair was sparse, topping a wrinkled, tanned face and the kindest dark eyes that Janet had ever seen. "Please come in—we'll start the ceremony right away. My housekeeper is a fine organist," he said, nodding toward the elderly Hawaiian lady at an ancient keyboard near the communion rail. Then he indicated a beaming middle-aged man coming up the walk behind them. "Kawika will be our other witness. He helps me to keep St. Andrews in order. I don't know how I'd manage without him."

"It's very kind of them both," Janet murmured.

"We're glad to do it." Father Lehua reached into the last pew and picked up a worn *Book of Common Prayer* as the woman at the organ started to play softly.

Janet felt Scott's firm clasp as they followed the elderly priest down to the altar. The ceremony that followed took on a dreamlike sequence; she was conscious of Father Lehua's liquid tones adding luster to the ages-old liturgy, the kindly expression on his brown face, the firmness of Scott's voice when it was time to repeat the vows, and the reassuring pressure of his fingers as she hesitantly made her response. Then the priest raised his right hand to proclaim the traditional blessing and she saw Scott bend his head. His light kiss landed at the corner of her lips while she stood woodenly, trying not to tremble. Mercifully, Scott seemed to understand because, as the organ

# THE CAPTURED HEART

swelled to a crescendo, he stayed close beside her, walking back down the narrow aisle.

There was another interval at the back of the church while they signed the church register, and Father Lehua added his signature to the official Certificate of Matrimony. She noticed Scott scanning that one carefully before nodding and putting it in his coat. Afterwards there was a brief flurry of hand-shaking with the witnesses on the outside steps, and she saw Scott press an envelope into the old minister's hands as the final good-byes were said.

Then they were back in the car and driving off. Janet waved from the car window until they turned onto the main road again, this time heading south.

She pulled off her hat and put it on the seat beside her. "They were all so *nice*. Everything about it was perfect." She clamped down on her lower lip to stop its trembling. "And I feel like such a fraud."

"I don't know why. Father Lehua didn't suspect anything. I just said we'd made up our minds in a hurry."

"He wouldn't have approved if he'd known the background," Janet persisted stubbornly. "We shouldn't have had a church ceremony."

"Don't be ridiculous—it can be dissolved just like any other." Scott's profile had its usual stony look. "We've bowed to the conventions—from now on, we can suit ourselves. Untying the knot, I mean."

"I know very well what you mean and you don't

have to sound so callous. It would be nice to salvage a few illusions."

"I'll be damned. If that doesn't beat all! Deliver me from a woman's mind. *You're* the one who was doing the complaining."

She subsided, as she recognized the validity of his objection. It was impossible to explain that the atmosphere for their brief ceremony had been so brimful of love and kindness that any kind of deceit seemed monstrous.

Her unhappiness must have made itself felt. There was an uneasy silence between them until Scott shifted behind the wheel and said, "Look, I'm sorry. I don't want to fight with you. Not today at any rate." His glance met hers as he smiled whimsically. "I guess we're both on edge."

"It was my fault." Janet decided to match his honesty. "You couldn't have found a prettier church if you'd searched all over the Islands. And now, believe it or not, I'm hungry. Did you say something about a picnic?"

"One picnic coming up," he said, following her lead. "Going back to the hotel for lunch seemed flat after . . . everything. There's a place not far away that overlooks Wainani Bay—I discovered the road by accident one day when I took a wrong turn."

"It sounds lovely." Her eyes teased him. "You're so good at planning these things that I'm beginning to wonder if you've had practice."

He grinned noncommittally. "If that's a subtle inquiry into my lurid past, I'll claim the Fifth Amendment. At least, you won't have to worry about any ex-Mrs. Fraziers. I didn't plan to get married for a few years." The last was added ruefully.

Janet felt he needn't have been so explicit. "Well, I didn't either. This whole affair is utterly ridiculous." As his grin broadened, she murmured, "Sorry, I forgot about our truce," and stared at the road ahead.

Scott slowed to avoid a pothole as he turned onto the narrow confines of a dirt road. "They could use some maintenance on this—I'd forgotten it was so rough. Somebody said it's mainly used for hauling cane." He gestured toward the sugar fields on either side of the car.

"They seem to go all the way down to the sea." Janet admired the tall stalks as they bent slightly with the breeze from the water.

"There's nothing else along here except a small private airfield. It was abandoned some years ago."

When they came to a fork in the road, Scott chose the steeper grade leading down to the water as cane fields on the right gave way to a rocky beach. The turbulence of the waves breaking upon the shore indicated a sharp drop-off to deep water beyond. It was a far cry from the broad, sandy beach at Kaiulani, Janet noted idly as he pulled up at the end of the road.

"On the rugged side, isn't it?" he said, turning off the ignition. "At least, we have it all to ourselves so I can get comfortable." He started to shed his tie and blazer as he spoke. "Too bad that you can't join the club."

Janet got out on her side. "You'll have to print some rules for your next wedding breakfast. How could I know that I was supposed to pack a swimsuit for a going-away outfit?"

"You have a point." Scott unbuttoned his collar before going around to open the trunk and lifting out a wicker hamper. "Shall we eat in the car or pick a nice soft rock?"

Janet's glance swept over the rugged beach with the sun beating on the dark sand. Then she looked down at her dress and made a gesture of surrender. "I'll take a raincheck on the rock."

"Okay," Scott moved the basket back to the wide front seat. "I prefer the creature comforts myself. Leave the door open for the breeze."

She nodded and slid back in the car, taking care not to bruise her flower lei against the seat. "Why don't you do the honors? I've suddenly decided I'm starving."

"Tomorrow I'll get you up for a proper breakfast in the dining room," Scott said as he opened the hamper and reached inside. "At the moment though, we have ham sandwiches with cheese or cheese sandwiches with ham. Take your choice."

"You're so good to me." She accepted one of the thick sandwiches and added, "I generally manage to find my way to breakfast without help. But thanks just the same."

"That was before you had a husband to watch over you."

"I don't need *anyone*—" she broke off as she saw his expression and knew that she'd risen to the bait once again. "What's in this?" she asked in confusion as he dropped a small foil package in her lap.

"Dill pickle . . . and a wedge of fresh pineapple."

"That's a strange combination."

"This is Hawaii." He put his sandwich on the dashboard and reached in the basket again. "I hope you like beer."

"Do I have a choice?" As he shook his head, her lips trembled with laughter. "Thanks, I'd love some."

"You can plan the menu next time." He watched her take a bite of pickle and frown slightly. "What's the matter?"

She took an exploratory taste of the pineapple spear before saying, "I can't decide which is worse—pineapple-flavored pickle or . . ."

"Pickle-flavored pineapple," he said, after taking a bite himeslf. "You're absolutely right. I suggest you skip both of them and concentrate on the sandwich."

After that, the time slid by pleasantly as they finished their sandwiches and lingered in conversation. The discussion ranged over food preferences where they discovered a mutual admiration for pastrami sandwiches and a shared aversion for snails and smoked oysters. From calories they went on to disagree mildly about American foreign policy, and skipped rapidly past politics to debate the merits of the Super Bowl versus the World Series. By the time they had found that Giacomo Puccini was their favorite operatic composer, with Wagner running a close second, the sun was halfway to the horizon.

"Where did the time go?" Janet asked when Scott looked at his watch and whistled with surprise.

"Damned if I know." He hastily gathered the remnants of their lunch back into the basket. "Why didn't you say something?"

She started to answer and then stopped, reluctant to admit that she'd been having such a pleasant afternoon that she'd forgotten all about time.

Scott closed his door and nodded for her to do the same before he turned on the ignition. They were halfway back to the main road before he spoke again. "I'm sorry I'll have to desert you for the rest of the day. One of our clients arranged a dinner meeting before all this came up."

"All this" meaning me, Janet thought, wondering why he suddenly sounded so stiff and unfriendly. As if he were heartily regretting the time they'd spent together.

"That's perfectly all right," she countered. "We agreed in the beginning to follow our original plans and there's certainly no reason to change."

"Umm." His grunt didn't reveal how he felt about that. He kept his attention on the road as it wound upward past the cane fields and the end of the deserter airport where a torn wind sock flapped on a ramshackle building. "What are your plans for the rest of the day?"

"I really hadn't decided." She could have pointed out that brides seldom planned extensive social schedules for their wedding night, but subdued the urge. "My report to Judge Byrne is overdue so I'd better get started on it. Don't worry about me."

"I wasn't. It just occurred to me that Marshall might wonder why I've left you alone again. Not that it's any of his business," Scott's voice was bitter, "but that doesn't stop him."

"Personally, I thought he was charming."

Scott's sardonic expression showed what he thought of her opinion. He braked forcefully at the highway before turning south toward Kaiulani. After that, the silence was unbroken all the way back to the hotel.

When they reached their room, Scott changed into a dark suit and was ready to go before Janet had time to put away her things.

His leave-taking was scarcely complimentary. "I'll try not to be too late," he said, halfway through the doorway. "Don't bother waiting up."

Despite her annoyance, Janet's lips curved slightly. If that wasn't a typical husbandly remark!

Scott must have realized it. He scowled and left without another word.

Janet walked out to sit on the lanai, trying to appreciate the colors in the sky as dusk descended. Then she got up again and moved restlessly into the bedroom. She stood looking at her briefcase on the desk and drummed her fingers on its cover. The proper thing would be to open it and get started on her report. She stared at it for another minute and then moved deliberately over to the telephone. She'd order dinner in her room and write to the Judge after that. Besides, the thought of eating by herself in the dining room held no appeal.

Then the sound of soft guitars starting to play on the terrace of the main building floated through the lanai screen. She lingered another minute before picking up the telephone and asking for room service. She'd placed her order and just hung up when the phone pealed. Wondering what she'd forgotten, she lifted the receiver again and heard Wayne Marshall's voice in her ear.

"Janet? I happened to be down here in the kitchen when they posted your order," he said after identifying himself. "You're not eating alone again tonight, are you? What's going on?"

"Nothing special," she said, carefully choosing her words. "Scott had a dinner meeting with a client."

"Well, we'd better have a dinner meeting, too." Wayne's pleasant voice had a grim undertone. "Actually, I tried to call you earlier. How about meeting me in the Batik Room in twenty minutes? I'll have a martini waiting."

For a second, Janet's conscience warred with her desire. Scott wouldn't be happy to hear that she'd had dinner with the publicity man again. On the other hand, she told herself, there was no reason for her to

THE CAPTURED HEART

go into hibernation because of some vows which she'd taken with her fingers crossed. Besides, if she provoked Scott enough, he might stay closer to home himself. That thought was inspiring enough to make her eyes gleam.

"Janet? Are you still there?" Wayne jiggled the phone impatiently.

"Yes, I'm here," she cut in before he severed the connection. "Twenty minutes will be fine, thanks. I'll hurry."

"And the martini?"

"That sounds fine, too," she said firmly before hanging up.

The decor of the Kaiulani's Batik Room was pure Arabian Nights fantasy. Red damask walls gleamed in the soft light provided by a huge brass candelabra hanging from the gold-colored ceiling. Banquette benches upholstered in a dark red batik print were complemented by low tables covered with the same material. The gleaming flatware atop them was gold-colored as were the beaten metal service plates.

A lovely Polynesian girl dressed in a golden sari met Janet as she paused in the entrance. "Mrs. Frazier? This way, please. Mr. Marshall is waiting for you at a table." She led the way to the bottom level of the dining room where Wayne was seated at a banquette by the window.

He stood to greet her. "Right on time. You're a woman in a million." His admiring glance went quickly over her brown chiffon blouse and long brown satin skirt. "I hope your husband appreciates how lucky he is."

"You'll have to ask him." Janet smiled her thanks at the hostess and sat down. "This is a gorgeous room . . . I suppose that curry is the only thing to order in these surroundings."

"Don't you believe it." He moved aside as a waiter wearing a white tunic and narrow pants put two iced martinis in front of them. "Despite the decor, this is the U.S.A. and I recommend the roast beef." He watched her pick up her glass and then raised his. *"Kipa hou mai!"*

She smiled at his careful pronunciation. "I'm impressed but illiterate. Translate it for me."

"I just said 'Come visit again.'"

*"Mahalo,"* she replied just as solemnly. "Now you've heard my entire vocabulary. I'll have to ask Thelma for another word or two."

Wayne's expression sobered. "You'll have plenty of time for that. More than you planned. That's what I wanted to tell you this afternoon. We've just received word that the ship carrying most of our exhibit was delayed by that typhoon off Okinawa. They're going to dock three days later than we scheduled. The opening will have to be postponed accordingly." He broke off at her frown and then went on. "Is it going to wreck your plans?"

"Well, I'm not sure what Scott will say." Janet lied, having a very good idea what his reaction would be.

Prolonging their stay together would irritate him still further.

"Don't look so grim. Most people would welcome the extra time at Kaiulani." The publicity man sounded offended. "The governor didn't seem to mind and even the ambassador went along with our date."

"I'm sorry. You just surprised me—that's all. For a second, I thought we'd have to change the dates on our mainland schedule."

"There's no reason for that. We'll shorten our preview here. Just keep your fingers crossed that the ship makes the new docking time."

"Without any more disasters," Janet agreed. "Would it help if I offered some berries to the local gods?"

He grinned and shook his head. "You're thinking of Madame Pele. She's goddess of volcanoes and concentrates on the eruptions of Mauna Loa. Typhoons are out of her province, I'm afraid. We have very specialized spirits around here."

"I'll remember."

"This time, put your money on the 'Kamakazi.'" He looked amused at her puzzled face. "Not what you're thinking. Our Kamakazi is the 'divine wind.' The islanders claim it destroyed the Mongol fleet years ago."

"Then it certainly should be able to handle the last end of a typhoon," she said smiling. "I'll remember when I mutter my incantations to the full moon."

"Fair enough. In the meantime, let's eat." He picked up an oversized menu and scanned it. "We'll have to keep our strength up with such a busy schedule."

Janet found herself thoroughly enjoying the lavish meal that followed. From the first course of lobster cocktail to the dessert of delicately frosted petit-fours, Kaiulani chefs had excelled. The service was efficient but unobtrusive, and when they were almost finished, the musicians started playing again on a neighboring terrace to add a final romantic touch.

Janet pushed aside her coffee and leaned back with a happy sigh. "This is the most incredibly beautiful place. It's almost unreal at night when you look out to see those gorgeous palm trees and that white sand beach."

"How about a stroll along that beach?" Wayne asked.

"I . . . I think not." She looked down at the tablecloth. "It's getting late."

"And besides, your husband wouldn't like it." There was rueful admiration in his tone. "You can't blame a man for trying."

"No—but it *is* your fault that I took that second petit-four," she said, changing the subject. "I'm so full that I can hardly move . . . let alone write any report."

"Join the crowd," Bonita Bristow said as she and her husband paused by their table. "I couldn't help overhearing."

As Wayne struggled to his feet, Janet tried not to stare at the outfits the Bristows were wearing. Bonita had donned a bare-midriff print of royal blue which would have been more flattering if she'd shed ten years or twenty pounds. Martin was in a striped suit and ruffled shirt of the same mod styling with a sequin tie which made Janet blink.

He saw her and grinned. "Pretty snappy, eh. Bunny picked it out for me—said it was the latest thing!"

"I thought you liked it," his wife protested, just catching the end of his comment.

"Baby, I like everything you do," he told her emphatically.

Janet felt a twinge of envy as she looked at them. Wearing a sequined tie was a small price to pay for such devotion.

"Can we buy you a drink?" Martin was going on.

Wayne glanced at Janet questioningly and she shook her head. "I couldn't consume another thing, thanks. Actually we were just leaving."

"C'mon, we can walk out together," Wayne said, holding out his hand to pull her up. Janet obediently tucked her purse under her arm and fell into step beside Bonita as they made their way toward the door.

"Is that good-looking husband of yours missing again?" the other woman asked, taking care that her words didn't carry to the two men behind them.

"He had an appointment. He's over here on business, so I can't complain," Janet explained lightly. "Lawyers are a serious breed."

"I'd say you were doing just fine with your second

Glenna Finley

team. It doesn't hurt to keep a man guessing now and then—although I'd never admit it to Martin."

Janet drew up outside the restaurant. "It isn't like that. I'm afraid you have the wrong idea."

"Says you." Bonita just winked before turning to include the men in her conversation. "What are you two looking so serious about?"

"Marshall was telling me that the art exhibit's been postponed," her husband said.

Bonita's cheerful expression faded as she stared at him. "Is that going to make a difference?"

"I've explained that Kaiulani can extend your room reservation—I'll handle it personally," Wayne said. "I hadn't realized before that you were such art enthusiasts."

"Martin is," Bonita said flatly. "I don't know one Buddha from another." There was an awkward silence until she went on. "Well, that means we'll all have to find something to fill the extra days. Maybe we can get Rodney to drive up to those volcanoes I was reading about."

Wayne nodded. "There's an orchid nursery in Hilo and a Macadamia nut factory, too. Most tourists take them in on the way."

Bonita didn't look enthusiastic. "It'd fill the gaps, I suppose. What have you planned?" she asked Janet. "Has your husband suggested anything?"

"He doesn't know about the postponement yet. The only thing I've arranged is a tour behind the scenes here in the hotel with Thelma Kahori."

## THE CAPTURED HEART

Bonita brightened. "That might be fun."

Janet nodded as they strolled slowly along the corridor toward the guest wing. "If enough employees speak English. Otherwise, we won't learn much."

"I must have missed out on something," Wayne complained. "Who doesn't speak English?"

"The maid who takes care of our room . . . for one."

"You're crazy," he said cheerfully. "All Kaiulani employees speak English. That's one of the conditions of employment here. Probably she's just shy. Some of the girls have never worked before—never even been out of their villages."

"You're lucky to get that kind of help," Martin put in. "At least you don't have to nail everything down around here."

Janet started to reply and then subsided as she met Wayne's troubled gaze. It was no time to be indiscreet. She pulled up as they reached the elevator and, turning to Wayne, held out her hand to him. "Thank you for dinner—it was delicious."

"My pleasure," he ignored the Bristows, who were looking on with unconcealed interest. "Sure I can't persuade you to take a walk on the beach?"

She shook her head regretfully. "If I got that close to the water, I'd want to go for a swim."

"At this time of night, you'd be better off in the pool," Martin put in.

"Don't tempt me or I'll never get any work done."

Janet smiled and shook her head. "See you all tomorrow. Good night."

When she arrived back at the room and found it still deserted, Janet wished that she hadn't been so firm in her refusal. She frowned as she picked up the travel clock and looked at the time. What kind of a dinner meeting lasted half the night? In all likelihood, Scott's business was concluded hours ago. Probably by now he was being royally entertained by some rancher's daughter or a whole covey of them.

The knowledge that she was being illogical and unfair in her reasoning made her more annoyed than ever. She put the clock down again and went in to the bureau.

She found her swimsuit in the layers of clothing and rummaged further for her cap. Darned if she'd stay here and go meekly to bed! A plunge in that gorgeous pool was something to do, at least. Something to pass the time so that she wouldn't be thinking about the dismal end of a day that had started with such promise.

As she donned her two-piece suit, she was glad that she hadn't told Wayne and the Bristows of her plans. At least, she wouldn't have to keep making excuses for an absent husband.

She shrugged into a thigh-length pool cover-up and picked up a towel before letting herself out of the door and locking it carefully behind her. Not that there was anything left to steal, she told herself wryly, and then bit her lip as she remembered that she still hadn't written to Judge Byrne as she'd planned. By now it had been so long that she'd have to break down and telephone him tomorrow.

Despite the hour, the building corridor was still adequately lighted, but the outdoor path to the pool that she turned onto was full of shadows. Tiny hooded lights placed at irregular intervals provided the bare minimum of illumination to indicate her route through the fragrant darkness.

Aside from the off-key note of an insect in the thick shrubbery alongside the walk, the stillness of the night was almost tangible. The crackling of a twig under her foot made her start nervously, and then, after shaking her head at her foolishness, she continued walking. While she hadn't expected crowds at the pool for a midnight swim, she hadn't realized the grounds of Kaiulani would be so completely deserted. Although she should have, she told herself, remembering the adage of resort hotels . . . "for the newly wed and nearly dead." The "nearly dead" at Kaiulani didn't waste their energy and the "newly wed" apparently ignored aquatic sports.

Of course, a missing bridegroom made a difference in some couple's lives. It forced a bride to cool off in the pool alone or spend a riotous night in her hotel room going steady with a crossword puzzle.

By the time Janet reached the darkened pool, she had run the gamut of emotions and was back to pure apathy. She tossed her towel on a nearby lounge and listlessly tucked her hair under her cap. A couple of laps would be enough exercise, she decided, wishing she'd just stayed in her room and gone to bed in the first place.

She moved down the broad tiled steps at the shallow end of the big free-form pool, guided by the faint underwater lighting. The warm water felt blissful on her skin as she struck out for the far side and felt it surge up over her shoulders. Perfume from the plumeria trees and the orange blossoms at the rim of the pool made a fragrant cloud as Janet surfaced and turned to float on her back. Overhead, a thin cloud cover shrouded the moon, allowing only a gleam of silver to escape from time to time. This was as thin as the intermittent breeze which fingered the surface of the pool. The setting was pure enchantment, Janet thought, admiring the silhouette of a bird-of-paradise planting.

She was so engrossed in her fantasy that a sudden splash in the darkness didn't register for a moment. By the time she was conscious of an intruder in the pool behind her and flailed the water to regain her balance, it was too late.

Two strong arms descended on her shoulders even as she opened her lips to cry out. She felt a strong thrust down and her scream was sliced off at the onset as her head went beneath the surface. She struggled angrily in protest and then, as the pressure on her shoulders didn't lessen, in panic and outright terror.

A panoply of thoughts flashed through her brain even as her fists battered against her attacker's chest

## THE CAPTURED HEART

and she kicked desperately to surface. Scott's face . . . the Bristows . . . even Wayne's countenance appeared in her vision—staring at her with dispassionate cruelty, watching her struggle from behind a safe barrier—immune to her desperate need for help.

For a split second, she broke free and shot to the surface. She gasped air into her bursting lungs before she was ruthlessly and abruptly dragged down again.

By then, her muscles had lost their strength and it was an effort even to move them. Her legs flailed weakly in the water; her head bobbed like a rag doll's against her chest. The faces in her vision faded as a merciful curtain of blackness descended. It took away all the pain and the terror—leaving a blessed void in its stead.

## Chapter Five

The newfound peace wasn't allowed to last. What followed was a new set of horrors.

Janet was dimly aware of a pressure at her back which crunched her ribs intermittently. As her circulation surged, her lungs burned and waves of nausea swam over her. Vainly she tried to retreat to the peaceful darkness but a stubborn voice lashed at her, pulling her back at every attempt.

Then she was appallingly sick, and afterwards pulled into a sitting position like a sack of grain. "That's the girl." The same voice jibed her. "Now—how do you feel?"

A low groan escaped her. "Go 'way," she managed before her eyes widened in sudden realization. "Oh, lord—I'm going to be sick again."

This time, she was conscious of a firm, comforting

hand at her forehead to ease her through that humiliating session. By the end of it, she was even aware of its identity. She turned her head to survey Scott irritably as he continued to kneel beside her. "What are you doing here?"

"If that isn't like a woman," his deep tone sounded rough. "Hells bells, I save your life and the first thing you do is complain about it."

"It's the second," she told him just as brusquely. "At first, I thought you were the one trying to push me under."

"Thanks a lot." He was hauling her to her feet. "If you can manage, I'll get you to the room and then call the doctor. There wasn't time before."

"My robe . . . it's around here someplace." She was looking around in bewilderment until the meaning of his words penetrated. Her head swiveled as she stared up at him. "You mean, somebody really tried to drown me? This wasn't a joke?"

"Damned right they did. By the time I got here, whoever it was beat it out the other side of the pool and disappeared into the shrubbery. You were at the top of the priority list right then, so I didn't have time for a second look." His voice was grim. "How do you feel now?"

She wrinkled her nose. "Don't ask . . ."

He stooped swiftly and gathered her in his arms. "That's what I was afraid of. I'll have you to the room in no time."

"Oh, really . . . I can walk." She tried to push out

of his firm clasp and felt his grip tighten instinctively.

"Cut it out! If you keep that up, the night watchman will think I'm abducting you," he protested.

"Where is he?" Janet turned to crane her head before letting it fall back against his chest as they turned into the building. Then she became conscious that the shirt under her cheek was damp and she raised her head again. "You're wet," she said accusingly. Her free hand went up to touch his sodden coat lapels. "And you've ruined your suit!"

Scott grunted. "What did you expect me to do—go back to the room and change?" He made an obvious effort to lighten his tone as he pulled up at their door and lowered her to her feet. "Besides, this is one of those wash-and-wear jobs—there's no harm done. Just stand there for a minute until I find the key," he instructed. "Okay—in we go."

Janet found herself shepherded into the room and lowered firmly onto the settee where she leaned back and closed her eyes. By then, she was beginning to tremble with cold and felt, rather than saw, a blanket put around her shoulders. Dimly she heard him at the telephone asking for the number of the medical clinic at Kohala. There were disjointed snatches of conversation before the overhead light was switched off, leaving only the soft glow of the desk lamp at the far side of the room.

"The doctor said to get you to bed." Scott was taking the blanket from her shoulders as he spoke and pulling her to a sitting position once again. "The

## THE CAPTURED HEART

most important thing is to keep you good and warm." He kept his tone impersonal and his hands moved deftly over her in the same way. Her swimsuit bra was removed and she was being toweled briskly before she even thought of protesting. By then, the sudden warmth felt so good that she meekly followed his instructions. When her skin was rosy with circulation, he put her into a cotton pajama coat, buttoning it beneath her throat before leading her over to the bed.

"This isn't mine," she murmured, feeling she should make a token protest, at least. "I have a nightgown in my suitcase . . ."

"That yellow chiffon with the ruffles? Very fetching but too drafty for tonight." He turned back the spread and pushed her briskly down onto the side of the bed. His head went up at a soft knock on the door. "That should be somebody from housekeeping with the hot water bottle."

"Whoever heard of a hot water bottle in Hawaii . . . ?"

He pulled the covers over her and moved to the door. "It's a first time for me, too. Stay put and stop complaining. You must be feeling better."

She watched him accept a hot water bottle from an older woman in a white uniform and closed her eyes as they held a low conversation. She opened them again at the sound of the door closing and watched Scott disappear into the bathroom, whistling softly.

There was only time to snuggle down into the sheets and think how nice it was to be cosseted like a baby, when he was back—pushing aside the sheet to place a carefully wrapped hot water bottle at her feet.

"Now all you have to do is go to sleep," he said, pulling the covers around her shoulders. "That was the hotel nurse I was talking to. She would have stayed"—as Janet stiffened, he went on quickly—"don't worry—I told her everything was under control."

"You didn't tell her anything else?" Janet was so tired she had trouble getting the words out.

"Just that you'd had an accident while swimming." He kept his voice noncommittal as he moved over to turn off the desk lamp, leaving only a faint illumination from the partially open bathroom door.

Janet made one last effort. "You won't go away? I'm sorry but I'd hate to be alone."

"I'll be here . . . don't give it another thought, honey."

He really would have to stop calling her by that absurd term, Janet thought, half-asleep already. She only managed to say, "I'm sorry that you have to be so uncomfortable . . ." before her eyelids went down to stay.

Scott stood quietly at her side for a moment or two, his expression hooded as he stared at the outline of her slight figure under the sheet. Then he rubbed the back of his neck wearily before going over to check the lock on the lanai door and get ready for bed himself.

In the hours that followed, Janet was conscious of

his reassuring tones when she suffered snatches of nightmares vivid enough to disturb her sleep. Once when she had tossed the bedcovers aside during such a bout, she felt them tucked around her shoulders again and heard a stern warning to keep them there.

When the morning sun filtered through the louvres of the lanai door, she awoke to discover how Scott had been able to be constantly at hand. His long length was stretched out under the sheet on the bed next to hers, leaving only the tops of bronzed shoulders and the back of his head visible to view.

She pushed up on an elbow to get a better look, thankful that he wasn't able to see the appalled surprise on her face. Thankful, too, that she had time for second thoughts about voicing her indignation at his presence. She lay staring at his powerful, relaxed form and felt a strange urge to go over and waken him; to run her fingers down . . .

She broke off—dismayed by the trend of her thoughts. Deliberately she pushed back the covers and stood up. Her reflection in the mirror across the room made her pause; the sleeves of Scott's blue pajama coat hid her hands and covered her slight frame to thigh level with tentlike proportions.

"I can't say much for the fit, but the color's great with your hair." Scott had punched a pillow up behind him and was surveying her dispassionately. "How do you feel this morning?"

"Er . . . much better, thanks." After determining that her robe wasn't within sight, she headed for the bathroom door, trying not to run. Scott's next comment caught her in mid-flight.

"Can you be ready for breakfast in fifteen minutes?"

She looked back, confused. "You mean, in the dining room?"

He yawned and sat up straighter. "I mean here ... I'll call room service now."

"All right," she tried to avoid looking at his bare chest as he reached for the phone, "but I'm not very hungry."

"I'll order something that slides down easily. Hurry up in there if you want me to shave before breakfast."

Her cheeks flamed at his casual warning. "I'd forgotten ... I mean, I'm not used to sharing ... I won't be long ..." She broke off in the middle of her explanation, to escape in indecent haste.

When she came back a few minutes later, she had donned a full-length caftan in shades of green which coincidentally was one of the most becoming items in her wardrobe. Scott had put on a matching dark blue robe over his pajama trousers and stood staring past the sunlit lanai to the beach below.

"I left your pajama top in the dressing room," she said, trying to sound as casual about the situation as he was. "If you don't need it, I'll have it laundered."

"No hurry ... I never wear it anyhow." He yawned and looked at his watch. "Finished in the bathroom?"

"Yes, thanks."

"Good." He moved past her to the door. "Shout when breakfast comes. I could do with some coffee."

She stood uncertainly in the middle of the room after he'd closed the door behind him and then checked her appearance in the mirror. It wouldn't have hurt him to say that she looked nice, she thought resentfully. Then she grimaced at her thoughts. Something about Hawaii was turning her into a simpering dolt.

By the time the room service waiter had arrived and deposited their breakfast on the lanai, she was able to knock briskly on the bathroom door. "Coffee's on."

"Go ahead and start—I'll be right there."

Scott had changed to sport shirt and slacks when he joined her a few minutes later. "This looks good," he said, picking up a glass of iced orange juice.

"It tastes good, too. I didn't think I was hungry."

"I remember." He spooned scrambled eggs onto a plate from an insulated casserole and added bacon. "You could do with some extra calories. And don't bother getting indignant," he added when her chin came up. "Save that for later when you explain what the hell you were doing in that swimming pool by yourself last night."

"I wasn't by myself . . . that was the trouble."

"Very funny. At least that means you're feeling better."

"What makes you think I have to explain anything to you?"

"I said . . . after breakfast," he informed her. "Otherwise you're apt to end up as the victim again. Any conversation before coffee is cause for justifiable homicide as far as I'm concerned. I remember a case in Chicago where the husband got off without even a reprimand from the judge."

"I never heard of such a thing," Janet began and then stopped as she caught sight of his amused expression. She laughed and picked up her knife. "You win. Pass the toast . . . will you, please."

Once they'd finished and were lingering over a last cup of coffee, Scott pushed his chair back into the partial shade of a philodendron, lit a cigarette, and surveyed her dispassionately. "Okay—now let's have it. What happened last night?"

"Nothing really. I had dinner in the Batik Room. Afterward the Bristows stopped by our table and . . ."

"*Our* table?" Scott scowled suddenly. "You didn't have dinner alone?"

Janet felt a twinge of guilt. "Wayne Marshall asked me to join him. You don't have to look so angry," she added. "All he wanted to do was tell me how the Exhibit's been postponed for a few days. Bad weather in the Pacific has delayed the shipment."

Miraculously, Scott's annoyed expression smoothed. "Then you'll have to stay on."

She decided he didn't have to sound so pleased

about it. "*I* will. It needn't affect your plans, though."

His look was noncommittal as he knocked some ash in a sand-filled saucer. "What happened after you met the Bristows?"

"We just saw them as we were leaving." She frowned as she tried to remember. "There was some talk about walking on the beach in the moonlight. Wayne invited me . . ."

"He did, did he?"

"Must you sound like a Puritan Father issuing orders for the day? I simply turned him down and came back to the room."

"Did you ever mention going swimming?"

"We may have discussed it . . ." She chewed on her lip as she tried to remember. "I honestly don't know." Her glance met his. "You think the attack was deliberate?"

"It had to be. The grounds here are fenced and the hotel has an elaborate security system. Plus the fact it's way to hell and gone away from everything. Hardly the place for anybody dropping in." Scott looked troubled as he ground out his cigarette. "I thought last night it was some drunken Casanova who was in the pool and got carried away."

Her blue eyes were scornful. "You might give me credit for some sense. I wouldn't have gone in the pool in the first place if it hadn't been deserted."

"That makes a lot of sense," he said sarcastically.

"What would have happened if you'd gotten a cramp?"

She stared at him. "Good heavens, I wasn't swimming the English Channel. You'll have ulcers before the month's over at this rate."

"That's all very well but you're still seeing a doctor when we go into Hilo this afternoon."

"But I feel perfectly fine this morning. Maybe a little tired . . ."

"That's not surprising. You had a hell of a night."

"So did you, I'm afraid." She realized that some thanks were overdue. "I hope you managed a little sleep."

"Enough. I'll drop in at police headquarters in Hilo while you're at the doctor's office. I know a fellow there—"

"But why see the police?"

"To make a few discreet inquiries about your friend Wayne Marshall, and the Bristows." Scott stood up and leaned against the lanai railing. "Something's beginning to smell fishy. Having our room rifled wasn't much, but this attack on you puts a different complexion on things." He moved to open the louvred screen behind her. "Better get dressed or I'll be short of time in Hilo."

Janet got to her feet. "I don't understand . . . what does that have to do with me?"

Scott spoke over his shoulder on the way to the telephone. "There wasn't time to tell you before—I have

## THE CAPTURED HEART

to fly into Honolulu this afternoon to get some information on a deed from the courthouse there."

"Oh—when will you be back?" Despite her intention, Janet's voice rose in dismay.

"Later tonight." He picked up the receiver. "I'll call now and see if Rodney can bring you back on his afternoon run. You won't want to hang around Hilo for hours waiting for me."

"No, I suppose not." Privately she was thinking it would have been nice if he'd asked her to go along. An afternoon shopping on Waikiki would certainly have been more fun than the schedule he'd announced.

Scott was watching her closely. "If you'd rather, I can try for another plane ticket, but I gathered you'd be busy with the Exhibit. Or does this postponement change things?"

Janet didn't intend to confess that she hadn't given a thought to her job since he'd loomed on the horizon. "Don't worry. I've millions of things to do," she announced airily. "When I get back from Hilo, I'll have to put in a call to Judge Byrne and bring him up to date."

"Wayne Marshall told me the Byrnes were spending the week on Long Island. He tried to call them the day we arrived."

"So that's why the Judge hasn't . . ."

". . . mentioned your transition to Mrs. Frazier. I imagine so. From what I hear, you're his pride and joy."

"He's been very good to me," Janet admitted.

Scott's jaw tightened. "Well, you can tell him about your marital problems later on."

After he'd finished checking with the hotel travel desk, he went over to take his coat from the back of a chair. "I'd like to leave in fifteen minutes."

"I'll be ready," she said, wondering if he always ran his life like the Long Island Railroad. "Aren't you going to take your briefcase?"

"Damn it all . . . yes!" He came back from the door and retrieved it from her, yawning hugely. "The way I'm functioning, I'll be lucky to find the airport."

"*I'm* the one going to the doctor."

He grinned wryly as he opened the door. "Maybe we should try for a group rate. I'll meet you up in the parking lot. And *don't*," he added sternly, "make any detours by the pool on the way."

Their drive down the scenic Hamakua coast to Hilo was a time of surprising enchantment as far as Janet was concerned. Scott's stiff manner faded as they drove past the famed Parker Ranch and he told how old-time ranchers held their roundups, island-style.

"They had to get the cattle out to the inter-island steamer when they sent them to market and that presented problems," he explained. "But then, the ranchers here were used to solving problems. It all started back in 1798 when Captain George Vancouver presented Kamehameha I with five cows and a bull.

## THE CAPTURED HEART

They were Spanish Longhorns from the missions in California. The ranch hands, or *paniolos*, came mostly from the Orient and had to be trained to the island life. Eventually they worked out a way for the seagoing roundups. The cowboys tied the cattle to lifeboats and swam them through the surf to the steamers where they would be taken aboard by slings. If any of their working horses submerged in the process and took in salt water, they were finished. An occupational hazard," he said wryly.

"But surely things have improved by now," she said, admiring the rolling green pasture land on either side of the road.

"There's no comparison. The Longhorn strain has changed to Herefords, Angus, and Brahma, and the ranchers have adopted a cow-calf operation with stock barged to feedlots in Honolulu for final fattening. On the other hand, the cowboys working these spreads still have names like Irving Chan, and the red sashes worn by Hawaiian musicians today are a throwback to the ones *paniolos* wore years ago."

Janet shook her head. "It sounds like Zane Grey with palm trees. I would never have believed it."

"You'd better. The biggest holding over here runs about fifty thousand head of cattle and has eight hundred horses. You can understand why they rank as valued clients for my firm." His expression sobered. "It might be better if you tagged along to Honolulu with me, though."

His offhand invitation stiffened Janet's feminine

pride. "I'll be perfectly all right back at the hotel. Besides, it wasn't in our arrangement that you had to serve as a 'round-the-clock guard.' " Deliberately she switched topics before he tried to change her mind. "Will it take us long to get to Hilo?"

His lips tightened but he didn't argue further. "It's a fair way. You'll enjoy the scenery once we get to the coast. There are wild orchids growing for miles along the roadside. Even wood roses and poinciana—I'll point them out for you."

An hour later on the winding road which had become crowded with traffic, he did just that. Besides the colorful flowers at the roadside, there were lush banana palms, breadfruit, and guava trees to border the unending fields of sugar cane. Scott slowed to show her some lauhala trees, whose fibers were used for weaving purses, and a few miles beyond, indicated a patch of Filipino bamboo orchids with tiny purple and white blossoms on their stalks. Their colors blended easily with the plumeria shrubs alongside whose flower clusters of yellow, pink, and white looked like dabs of paint against the pale blue sky.

"In the Far East, they identify plumeria as 'frangipani' or 'temple flower,' " Scott explained. "These days they're the commonest flower for Hawaiian leis."

"Don't forget putting them on pillowcases at night. There's probably some story behind that. It's too bad we can't ask the maid."

"Why not?"

## THE CAPTURED HEART

"The communications gap—remember? Thelma claims the girl doesn't speak English."

Scott looked puzzled. "You've lost me."

"Well, Wayne said that all the Kaiulani employees speak English, but I didn't argue with him. Maybe the maid was a friend of Thelma's who needed work." Janet's eyes narrowed in concentration. "Although I could swear I've seen her before . . . somewhere."

"Umm." Scott sounded doubtful. "You were wise not to pursue it. Jobs are at a premium over here—probably there was some hanky-panky in the hiring."

She nodded. "It doesn't matter to me as long as she does her job and scatters enough plumeria blossoms behind. They're better than rose petals."

"That proves you're a *malihini*. When the plumeria plants were first brought to the Islands, they were planted almost exclusively in cemetaries. The natives avoided using them for anything else."

"More island taboos?"

"So I've read. There were a lot of them; in those days, men wouldn't eat in the company of women or cut a single tree without asking permission of the Forest God first. Even on my last trip here, I heard the story of a family who transferred some stones from a *heiau* or shrine to their front walk. Apparently, the stones put up such a plaintive wail each night that they finally returned them so they could get some sleep."

"And nothing dastardly happened to them?" Janet

asked, wanting him to continue in the relaxed, friendly tone he'd adopted.

"They're still perfectly healthy." He grinned. "At least, they didn't have to go to the 'City of Refuge' over on the Kona coast."

Janet frowned as she tried to think. "I've heard that name, but I can't remember where."

"Over here, the City of Refuge was like home base on a baseball diamond. If a native managed to reach that part of the island, all his crimes were forgiven. The best part was that the offenders didn't even have to stay there. The priests absolved them after a few days and they simply walked out—free as a breeze. Rodney Kahori can tell you more about it this afternoon when he takes you back to Kaiulani; he knows most of the stories on island folklore. Incidentally, he'll be expecting you at the airport by the inter-island desk about three this afternoon unless you change plans." Scott braked and swore sharply as a passing car cut in front of him. "Damn! A few feet closer and we'd both have been seeing a doctor in Hilo."

"I still don't understand why I have to go . . ."

"There's no sense taking any chances," he informed her autocratically. "Later on, you can tour the town. There's a new shopping center that went up after the tidal wave of 1960 wiped out a third of the city. It's almost as good as Waikiki. Afterwards, you can lunch on Teriyaki Milk."

Her eyebrows went up at his teasing. "I'll ask for a

## THE CAPTURED HEART

double portion. Will you be late getting back from Honolulu?"

"I might be. Depends on what plane connections I can make at the last minute." He added, sounding irritable again, "For God's sake, use your head tonight and stay in the room until I get back."

It would have been nice, she thought as she looked determinedly out the car window, if he'd stop acting like an angry den father every time he told her what to do.

Scott's jaw was still tight when he dropped her in front of a modern professional building in Hilo a little later. "The hotel down by the park is a good place for lunch," he told her as she got out of the car, "and there shouldn't be any trouble picking up a cab to take you to the airport."

"Thanks, I'll be fine." Janet kept her tone airy with an effort. "Have a good time in Honolulu."

"I wouldn't be going if it weren't for this damned deed."

"You don't have to keep explaining." She hesitated before closing the car door. "I suppose it will be a while before the police can give any information?"

Scott nodded. "That's why I said to watch your step. I'd better leave," he added pointedly, "or I'll miss my flight."

Janet managed to close the door without slamming it, but it was an effort. She watched him drive away and tried to ignore the empty feeling that settled over her.

The doctor was a brisk middle-aged man who shook his head and frowned when she told of her experience the night before. After examining her, he ordered a regime of rest and relaxation. "You can't overlook the shock to your nervous system," he said in fatherly tones. "Tell that husband of yours that I said you were to be pampered—not that he doesn't seem to be trying. He certainly sounded concerned when he arranged your appointment."

"He's been very nice," Janet murmured.

"Newlyweds, I'll bet. Well, it was a damnable thing to happen on a honeymoon," he said, going back to sit behind his desk.

Which was an understatement if she'd ever heard one, Janet decided as she left his office a few minutes later. She aimlessly followed the street signs down to the lush greenery of Liliuokalani Park with its Japanese bridges and leaned over a stone parapet to stare at the still pond water beneath. If she faced facts, it had been a damnable honeymoon even before the incident in the swimming pool. A platonic marriage was about as much fun as Russian Roulette and equally dangerous. Her eyes darkened as she let her thoughts dwell on Scott. He would turn out to be the most attractive male she'd ever met. If only they'd seen each other again in New York under other circumstances, their acquaintance could have developed normally. But now—there wasn't any chance at all. Thrown into a false intimacy from the outset, it was

# THE CAPTURED HEART

small wonder that Scott persisted in treating her like one of the knots on the family tree.

A tiny bird landed on the bridge railing next to Janet's hand and chirped inquiringly. She smiled at it, deciding it was time to move on and order some lunch before she started telling her troubles to anyone who would listen.

She found Rodney by the station wagon at the Hilo airport later that afternoon. By then, the heat had reached broiling temperature and the metal roofs on the hillside houses looked like bright mirrors as they reflected the sun's rays against the thick green vegetation framing them.

Rodney was as imperturbable as ever in a pair of shorts and a bright print shirt. "You're right on time," he told Janet approvingly. "Mr. Frazier was afraid you wouldn't make it."

"Mr. Frazier worries too much." She folded her cotton blazer on the front seat and dropped her purse beside it. "Do we have to wait for anybody on that California plane that just landed?"

"Not today . . . you're my only passenger." Rodney held the car door for her. "Hop in and we'll leave right away."

Once they left the bustling traffic of the airport, he announced they were taking the scenic route back to Kaiulani. "You should see the banyan trees by the waterfront which were planted by our well-known visitors. Amelia Earhart even planted one just before her plane was lost in the Pacific. After that, we'll go past the park——"

Janet interrupted him. "Could we do it another time . . . please, Rodney. Right now, I'd like to go straight back to the hotel. It's been a long day and I don't need any more sightseeing."

He looked away from his driving long enough to give her a curious glance. "What's the matter, Mrs. Frazier? Don't you feel well? Maybe this sun's too much for you, huh?"

"I'm expecting a long-distance call late this afternoon," she told him, crossing her fingers under the edge of her skirt. "I told my husband I'd be back in plenty of time."

Rodney's face fell. "I thought you'd like a personal tour of Akaka Falls on the way north. It's not far off the highway."

"Not today." Janet's tone was polite but firm. "Straight back to Kaiulani, please." She leaned back, closing her eyes to discourage any more discussion from the eager young driver, and fell sound asleep in the process.

She didn't waken until Rodney braked the station wagon to turn off the highway into Kaiulani's curved drive and, by then, felt so guilty about turning down his tour-guide overtures that she overtipped him handsomely when she got out of the car.

His eyes lit up as he saw the denomination of the bill. "Maybe you'd like to drive to the Falls tomorrow, Mrs. Frazier . . . or how about the Macadamia

Nut factory . . . or the orchid plantations on the way to the volcanoes . . ."

She stopped his sales talk before he could include a complete outer-islands tour plus a side trip to Disneyland. "I'll have to wait and see what happens, Rodney."

"I told Mr. Frazier I'd be glad to take you whenever he was working," he persisted. "He's a pretty busy man when he visits the Islands, I hear. Guess he's been entertained by some of the big families."

Janet secretly wished she had his sources of information to satisfy her curiosity about Scott but knew better than to encourage further gossip. "Thanks for picking me up today—I appreciated it."

"Any time, ma'am." Rodney grinned and managed a creditable Oriental bow before getting back in the car and cheerfully driving off.

Janet watched him go and turned toward the lobby. Rodney was certainly avid for extra work. The only thing he'd missed was Robert Burns's famous line—"Whistle and I'll come."

It was a shame that Scott didn't read Burns's poetry as well, she decided. If her husband ever put those words to the test—he'd find he didn't even have to whistle.

## Chapter Six

Fortunately Janet's ancestors had endowed her with a liberal quantity of common sense as well as striking red hair. There was no sense mooning around like a Victorian heroine in the last throes, she told herself severely, and made up her mind to enjoy the rest of the evening.

Room service provided a delectable dinner which she consumed out on the lanai with a hurricane lantern on the table and the fabulous Hawaiian moon as an overhead fixture. Afterwards, she reread the Exhibit catalogue; a task long overdue. Her conscientious struggle with the biographical data on Buddha and Suyra, the Hindu sun god, made her decide to relax in a warm bubble bath afterwards. Scott had forbidden the swimming pool, but he'd find nothing to complain about in her behavior this time.

# THE CAPTURED HEART

Janet hummed softly to herself as she dumped a generous capful of pink geranium fragrance in the warm water and then unpacked a green and black robe. She surveyed its ruffled cowl collar and cuffs with satisfaction as she reached for a nightgown of matching green. The latter was a sleek Empire design except for a sheer chiffon inset at the waist. It had been a wildly extravagant purchase the month before and had been tucked into her suitcase at the last minute.

Janet hung her finery in the bathroom and relaxed in the warm water under a frothy layer of bubbles. As the minutes went by, she regulated the temperature by turning on more warm water with her toes while she lay with her eyes closed—putting off the moment of emerging.

The first faint sound from the bedroom didn't even penetrate. It took the abrupt opening of the bathroom door to make her eyes flash open with alarm. When she saw Scott's tall figure striding toward her across the room, she surfaced like a startled dolphin. "What are you doing here . . ." she began.

"You'd better ask." Scott pulled up at the side of the tub and stared balefully down at her. "Of all the damn-fool capers—this one really takes the cake! I've been all over this hotel looking for you. It never occurred to me that you'd be lying in here with every door unlocked. Why didn't you throw out the welcome mat and some rose petals while you were about it."

A draft of cold air from the air-conditioned bedroom hitting Janet's bare shoulders indicated that her bubble camouflage had slipped drastically. She gasped and hastily slid back down into the water. "I don't know why you're complaining. I did everything you told me to—I had dinner alone . . ."

"Well, that's a switch."

"But now I don't know why I bothered. You come charging in here to read the riot act without even knocking . . ."

"Do you think the guy who tried to drown you in the swimming pool would bother to knock?" His scathing gaze swept her inch by inch. "I must say you make it easy."

"But I *did* lock the door. I'm sure I did." For the first time, her tone wobbled uncertainly as his words sunk in. "Unless the maid came in or the room service waiter left it unlocked."

"Or fish could fly." He raked a hand through his hair. "Why don't you just admit that maybe once—just once—you made a mistake."

Her chin went up, barely clearing the bubbles. "I've no intention of it. And you can leave any time. You don't have the right to complain about everything I do."

"I have a whole basketful of rights," he snapped, "any damned time I choose to use them. You'd better start remembering that."

"I had . . . had I!" Janet was so angry that she was almost sputtering. She would like to have

# THE CAPTURED HEART

stormed to her feet and ordered him from the room with a regal gesture. That possibility was clearly impossible, but as she moved in frustration, she felt a sodden bath sponge touch against her wrist under the bubbles. The next thing she knew, she had grabbed it and let fly.

The soaking mass hit the middle of Scott's immaculate silk necktie and dropped at his feet with a noisy plop. He stared unbelievingly at it for a second, and then brought his flaming glance up to meet hers.

Without saying a word, he stooped to retrieve the soggy sponge and the next minute he was standing beside the tub, squeezing it over her head.

"*Stop* that!" she shrieked, sitting up and trying to shield her head from the soapy deluge. "Oh, look at my hair!"

"I am." Scott calmly dropped the wrung-out sponge back into the tub and dried his hands on a bath towel. "You'd better do something about it. But don't get any more bright ideas," he added calmly as he saw her fists clench. "Try tossing that bath sponge around once more and you'll get more than you bargained for."

"If that's a threat . . ."

"I'm just warning you. Start acting like a wife and you'll be treated like one." His eyes glinted dangerously. "Only next time we'll choose a different playground and *I'll* make the rules."

"You wouldn't dare!" Despite her bravado, Janet heard her voice tremble.

"No?" Scott brushed down his tie with the back of his hand and tossed her the towel before going over to the dressing room door. "I'm going to get ready for bed. Knock when you're through in here."

Janet clutched the towel to her, vainly trying to keep it from sagging in the bath water. "I don't know why it matters since you're going to spend the night in there."

He stopped halfway through the dressing room doorway and stared at her with undisguised amusement. "Stay in here again? You must be dreaming. Our marriage license may have saved your reputation but as far as I'm concerned, it guaranteed me a decent bed."

"In that case, *I'll* sleep in the dressing room."

Her retort stopped him halfway through the door. He shrugged again. "Suit yourself, but I should warn you that the air-conditioning is colder than Nome in winter. You'd better call the housekeeper for a couple more blankets and get that hot water bottle back again."

Janet wasn't entranced at explaining such a need to a Hawaiian housekeeper. She felt the end of her towel slip farther into the water and wondered if she were going to have to spend the entire night sitting in the bathtub. Only stubborn feminine pride made her persist in her argument. "I'll sleep out on the lanai then. That lounge looks perfectly comfortable."

"Better you than me." Scott yawned and started to

close the dressing room door. "I just hope it doesn't rain."

"If it does, I'll extend the awning," she said smugly.

"Well, suit yourself." His tone didn't give any indication of his feelings. There was nothing indecisive about the way he slammed the door, however, and Janet wore a look of triumph when she finally climbed out of the tub. It had been a strange battlefield but, for once, she'd won.

It wasn't until the rains came at three o'clock in the morning that she had to admit she was wrong again. The first whisper of water on the stiff palm fronds ringing the lanai made her waken instantly, only to smile as the rain continued. Before going to bed, she had pushed the lounge under cover so that her blanket would stay snug and dry. A few minutes later, however, she found disaster had arrived from another source; the rivulets of water had scarcely stopped draining from the lanai's greenery when an all-too-familiar whine sounded beside her ear on the pillow. Within two minutes, the battle cry of mosquitos was loud enough to signal regimental strength.

A mad slapping session ensued without notable success. Finally, she pulled the blanket over her head, deciding suffocation would be better than being devoured by the winged attack forces.

It only took five minutes of that before she came out from under the blanket to beat a rapid retreat into the bedroom.

"Make sure that screen's closed!" Scott rapped out as soon as she was inside the room, still panting from her exertions. "Otherwise they'll be all over the place."

Janet followed his instructions while he leaned over and switched on the bed lamp. She glanced angrily over her shoulder at him once she'd secured the latch on the screen. "Why didn't you tell me that I'd be eaten alive out there?"

He propped himself up against the headboard and stared back at her. "You didn't ask. Besides, the mosquitos only come out after it rains." As she stood uncertainly by the doorway, he checked his watch under the lamp and slid back down under the sheet. "Get some sleep or you'll be a wreck in the morning. There's another blanket in the closet if you need it."

She watched him pull his own blanket up over a bronzed shoulder and decisively turn his back on her. For a moment she just stood there, weighing what her next move should be. Then sheer weariness outweighed all other considerations and she padded over to the empty bed beside him to turn back the covers. The time for protest was past. She slid between the sheets and reached out to turn off the lamp, yawning mightily all the while.

Her final act was to cast an annoyed look at the long, motionless figure in the next bed. It was one thing for a man to keep his distance, but another thing entirely to be so damned detached that it was an insult to the entire feminine sex!

## THE CAPTURED HEART

By the next morning, Scott had evidently decided that a truce was the safest course to follow. Over breakfast on the lanai, he exhibited a careful indifference to her green and black ruffled robe and merely mentioned she should find something to put on the mosquito bite on her wrist that she had scratched in a forgetful moment.

"It's perfectly all right," she snapped back, before remembering she too was going to try different tactics in the light of day. Hastily she sipped her coffee and tried to sound cool and serene. "You didn't tell me what you learned in Hilo yesterday."

A flicker of a smile went over Scott's tanned face. "There wasn't time last night. We were too busy discussing other things." Then, as her eyebrows climbed warningly, he said, "It wasn't a complete report by any means . . . simply a preliminary one. I phoned headquarters before I left Honolulu. Hilo had just received a cable a few minutes before. Wayne Marshall's perfectly clean . . ."

"I *thought* so," Janet told him with perverse satisfaction.

"I merely stated there was nothing in his past history to show a fondness for drowning redheads in swimming pools. Possibly it's a recently acquired taste."

She glared across the coffee pot at him. "The man's been a perfect gentleman."

". . . unlike some others you could mention."

"Stop trying to lead your witness, Mr. Frazier. Don't forget I've been around lawyers before."

"A fact that I'm doing my best to forget." He helped himself to a cigarette and lit it. "Where were we?"

"Talking about Wayne Marshall . . ."

"Ummm." Scott disposed of his match in the ashtray and leaned back in his chair. "Well, if Marshall came out sunny-side up, Bristow wasn't quite so lucky. According to the police, he's been connected with some shady deals in the past." At Janet's indrawn breath of surprise, he added, "Nothing like the swimming pool thing, though. Martin got his start in con rackets. After that, he was reported to be involved with the syndicate people in New Jersey, but was never convicted. Then, he seems to have pulled out and tried for something with less risk. According to the mainland authorities, these days he's importing Oriental art."

"That checks. It was the Exhibit that brought him to Kaiulani in the first place. He said so on the ride from Kona."

Scott scratched the side of his nose. "Hardly the type to go after a woman in a swimming pool. Unless it was a fit of passion . . ."

Janet broke into laughter. "For me! Hardly. He's absolutely devoted to Bonita. This is a second honeymoon for them."

"They haven't been married all that long," Scott said in a dry tone. "Bonita's had other business interests."

"Well, she's concentrating on Martin now," Janet

insisted. "Anybody could see that." She leaned on the table and rested her chin on her hand. "Actually, we haven't learned a thing, have we?"

"Just that Martin Bristow would have a good reason for wanting to see that Exhibit list with the valuations on it. But there isn't a shred of evidence to connect him with the disappearance."

"And stealing an insurance list isn't a federal case. If something disappears after the Exhibit opens . . ." her voice trailed off.

"That's different." Scott grinned wryly. "You sound just like my pal down in police headquarters. All he could suggest was that you avoid any midnight swims and advised keeping your eyes open while we're here."

Janet got abruptly to her feet and walked over to the lanai railing to stare down at the sunlit beach. "I've dragged you into an awful mess. Ever since I've set foot on this island, I've felt like a millstone around your neck. Everything's going wrong."

"That's absurd. I was beginning to think there were some decided advantages . . ."

She glanced over her shoulder. "There's no use joking about it. You know very well that you had no idea what you were getting into."

"That's true enough."

Janet's cheeks reddened at his rueful expression. "What I'm trying to say," she managed with some difficulty, "is that I think you should go on with your original plans. If anybody asks questions, you can say that your firm called you home."

"But they haven't. After the trouble I had at the courthouse in Honolulu yesterday, I'll have to stay in the Islands longer than I planned. That deed my client filed isn't worth the paper it's written on." Scott got up lazily and moved over to the railing beside her. He put a finger under her chin and forced her to meet his amused eyes. "So I suggest you stop being virtuous about this whole affair and relax. I'll even bare my soul and admit that I seldom do anything I don't want to."

She felt more embarrassed than ever by his kindness. "Something tells me you're an awful liar."

"Nothing of the kind," he replied stoutly. "It's obvious you don't know much about the male sex. Pure gold in most respects but self-centered as hell." He put his hands on her shoulders and pointed her toward the bedroom. "Go get some clothes on. I like that ruffly thing, but the tourists at Volcano House might stare."

"Volcano House? You mean now? I haven't arranged a trip there."

Scott moved over to the table to extinguish his cigarette. "*You* haven't," he said casually, "But I have. Nobody comes to the big island without paying their respects to Madame Pele. Rodney will have a car for us around front at nine thirty."

"Rodney?" Janet knew she sounded like an idiot, parroting his words.

The same thought evidently occurred to Scott. He

## THE CAPTURED HEART

propelled her into the bedroom none too gently. "You're beginning to sound like a zombie. More sleep for you tonight, lady. Playing musical beds doesn't agree with you."

For a second, she stiffened but her defenses folded abruptly. There was no point in spoiling the day by arguing; besides she was aware that he was right. Aside from her mosquito bites, she was still stiff from trying to get comfortable on the lanai lounge. Conventions could go by the board from now on, she told herself, and marched obediently toward the dressing room.

When they met Rodney standing beside a Kaiulani station wagon in the curving drive, they found that their plans for the day had been altered slightly. He waved a hand toward Martin and Bonita who were already ensconced on the rear seat. "The Bristows had trouble with the brakes on their rental car so they asked if they could hitch a ride with us. I was sure you folks wouldn't mind since we were all going to the same place."

"Of course not," Scott's response was prompt, but Janet was aware of the slight tightening of his jaw. As she echoed his denial, she hoped her words didn't sound as hollow as they were.

She got into the front seat of the car and managed to say all the conventionally proper things to the Bristows while her mind pursued another tangent entirely. What rotten luck to have their whole day's outing changed, she was thinking. After it had started out so well, too. Now—instead of having a chance to spend the day with Scott, she was plunged into an unwilling foursome. A second look at the Bristows' faces had shown that they weren't enchanted by the gathering of the clans either. Only Rodney, whose take-home pay for the day would be sizable, looked like a satisfied Buddha as he slid in the driver's seat.

"That damned car of ours," Martin was grumbling as they drove off. "I knew yesterday something was going wrong with the brakes. I almost had to drag my feet to make the turn into the hotel last night."

Bonita was checking her makeup in an oversized compact mirror. "I don't know why you're fussing. We'll see the volcanoes, after all. Frankly, I could have used a day on the beach," she confided to Janet, "but Martin isn't happy unless he's dragging me from one thing to another. I've worn out a pair of shoes already."

"I like keeping busy." Martin sounded both apologetic and defiant. "When I was growing up, I didn't have enough money to take a vacation. Now"—he gestured derisively down at his flamboyant sports clothes —"I have all the trappings and I don't give a damn."

Despite all she'd heard of his background, Janet couldn't help admiring his honesty. From the fond look on Bonita's face, she was feeling the same way.

"It's time somebody pounded some learning in my noggin," she told Janet. "People have been trying for years and it's never made a dent." Leaning forward, she put a manicured hand on the seat and said,

"You'll have to tell me about where we're going, Rod. What's the scoop on this Pele I've been hearing about?"

Rodney grinned good-naturedly at her in the rearview mirror. "You'll be visiting at her home when we get to Kilauea Crater. Madame Pele, as we call her, is the Hawaiian goddess of fire, so nobody wants to rile her unnecessarily. That's why they still make offerings to her during Aloha Week. Don't forget," he added solemnly, "Mauna Loa still rumbles, and the lava flows on our south coast are proof of Madame's power."

Bonita's thin eyebrows arched. "I *am* impressed."

"Well, I'm glad you're finally listening," her husband put in. "You weren't paying any attention when I was reading the guidebook last night."

"Who wants to listen to statistics on a terrace in the moonlight?" she replied, undaunted. "Besides, that wasn't about Pele."

"Mauna Kea's the other volcanic cone over here," Martin said patiently. "I think they said it was the world's tallest mountain. Is that right?" he asked Rodney.

"If you measure from the base on the ocean floor, Mauna Kea's over thirty-three thousand feet. That's four thousand more than Mount Everest in the Himalayas."

Bonita wrinkled her nose. "Sounds a little snitchy to me."

"We have some very energetic publicity men over

here," Rod admitted. "They try to earn their salaries."

Janet felt Scott move on the seat beside her and knew what he was thinking. Unfortunately, Rodney chose that moment to say, "That reminds me, Mrs. Frazier—Wayne Marshall wants you to get in touch with him when you get back. Said he'd made some plans for you tomorrow."

Bonita gave a gurgle of laughter. "Rodney, you'll never learn." She eyed Scott's stony profile mischievously before going on. "If you want to get ahead in the world, you'll have to be more diplomatic. Never, *never* say a thing like that in front of a woman's husband."

"Bunny, behave yourself," Martin growled. He shook his head and muttered apologetically to Scott. "Women!"

Janet could have killed them all. "Wayne probably wants to report the latest news about the Exhibit opening. There was still some doubt about the freighter's docking time when I talked to him."

"I hope to God the date hasn't been postponed again," Martin muttered. "Fun's fun . . . but I can't spend the month over here. I won't have a business to go back to."

Bonita's good-natured features took on a worried cast. "Let's not get back on that subject." She made her voice light. "Rodney, tell us more about Madame Pele. I like the sound of the old girl."

"Believe me, she's had her moments," their driver

said ruefully. "Things are pretty quiet now, but there have been lava flows all over the south part of the island. As a matter of fact, the Puna flow is still letting off steam and heat—once you get to the Halemaumau Firepit, you'll see the lava bubbling today."

"There's no chance of it spilling over, is there?" Bonita asked.

"These days the scientists give plenty of advance warning," he assured her. "You won't have to leave your footprints in the warm lava like our ancestors."

The older woman shuddered. "That's a blessing. All I want to do is see the place, take a few pictures, and eat lunch."

"There's a good spot for that," Rodney said. "Afterwards, there'll be time for a walk along the nature trails. It gives you a chance to trace the old flows and the vegetation."

"Is it dangerous?" Bonita persisted.

"Bunny . . . for pete's sake!" Martin began.

Rodney cut in cheerfully. "Only if you get off the paths, Mrs. Bristow, and you don't look like the type for a sacrifice to Madame Pele."

"Hardly." Bonita considered his remark a minute and then asked, "Did they really throw women into the crater in the old days?"

His features became impassively Oriental. "All the Polynesians had their *kapus*; it's not for us to judge their reasons. Even today, it's best not to inquire too closely." His eyelids flickered. "Or to condemn, I think."

After that, it was quieter than usual for the rest of the drive down the scenic coastline and through the bustling streets of Hilo. Once they left the city limits, the road started climbing upward, skirting the foothills of Mauna Loa.

The thick tree ferns beside the highway still glistened with raindrops—a tangible reminder from the gray clouds now scudding across the sky toward the Kona coast. The fern fronds provided a lacy canopy as they emerged from their base of dark soft *pulu* which, Rodney explained, provided stuffing for pillows and mattresses.

"Nothing is wasted in the Islands," he went on. "We use the *hapu'u* or base for our carved Tiki gods. The smaller ones are sold for orchid logs. Our eucalyptus trees have lots of uses, too. Did you know they called them 'Ward Off Fever' trees in the old days? And when they didn't grow them for medicine, they used them for timber and gum."

"I'll have to hand it to you, Rodney," Bonita said. "There's not much you've missed in this guidebook stuff. Maybe you could tell us what to have for lunch when we get up to Volcano House."

"You're on your own there. I always bring a sandwich from home. With my wife's medical bills piling up, I have to cut corners."

"How much time will we have after lunch?" Martin was asking. "I want to get some pictures."

"I'd planned on about two hours before we start

## THE CAPTURED HEART

back," the driver said. "What did you want to do, Mr. Frazier?"

"The usual thing, I guess." Scott looked at Janet for confirmation and then went on. "Take a walk . . . look at the crater . . . two hours should be plenty."

Rodney nodded. "Everything's okay, then. You won't have any trouble on your own; there are two or three nature trails that start from the park headquarters."

"I'm not going far on these." Bonita was ruefully surveying her platform sandals.

Martin gave her shoulder a reassuring squeeze. "That's okay. We'll be able to see plenty at the museum. You can sit and watch the color movies. The park people have something for everybody."

His prophecy turned out to be accurate. After depositing them at the entrance of the restaurant located on the very brim of the Kilauea Volcano area, Rodney pointed out the park buildings nearby and promised to reclaim them in the middle of the afternoon, before driving off.

"Probably he'll eat his sandwich and then take a nap somewhere in the shade," Martin muttered. He gestured them ahead of him, into an attractive large restaurant-hotel constructed of dark native stone.

"You can't blame him," Bonita said. "He's probably made this trip so often that he could drive the road in his sleep." She led the way through the foyer into a spacious glass-fronted lobby overlooking the massive gray lava area with the still-smoking Halemaumau Crater in the distance. Her eyes widened. "I didn't know it was so big! It's sort of like seeing a movie of the moon's surface on a wide screen." She reached to grasp her husband's hand. "C'mon, let's eat. If I stare at that very long, Madame Pele will spoil my appetite."

After they all consumed a well-prepared lunch—which proved that Madame Pele hadn't bothered to work any of her spells—the Bristows headed for the Volcanological Museum in the park headquarters, wrangling amiably whether to shop for souvenirs before or after the color movie.

Scott watched them go, and then glanced down at Janet. "Alone at last," he quoted with amusement. "So much for all my plans."

Her eyes crinkled with laughter. "It turned out pretty well . . . all things considered. I think the Bristows were just as appalled as we were when we left the hotel."

"Rodney should advertise group rates for honeymoons." Scott's expression was wry as he took her elbow and steered her around the end of the building. "I'm beginning to think I'll have to make an appointment if I ever want to catch you alone."

"*You've* been a little hard to find, yourself," Janet pointed out. She tried to keep her voice calm although her heart had suddenly tripled its beat. "What with business dinners and trips to the courthouse in Honolulu."

## THE CAPTURED HEART

"You've got me there—guilty as charged," he admitted. "My only defense is that I didn't know I'd have a wife in the background when I set up the schedule."

"Oh, I wasn't criticizing . . ."

"But now I've been able to shift things around a little," he went on in a satisfied tone, ignoring her interruption. "Business can wait."

"There's no need for you to change anything . . ."

"I wish to God you'd stop saying that. When will you get it into your head that maybe I *want* to?"

"Well, how was I to know?" she flared without thinking. Then her voice faltered as she met his eyes. "This is the first I've heard."

For an instant, the background noises faded into oblivion for both of them. The sun went unnoticed as it emerged from the clouds to spread its warm rays over them before disappearing abruptly again.

Finally the sound of a truck back-fire from the highway managed to penetrate the interlude. Janet stepped back and put up a hand to smooth her hair, still feeling strangely bemused and flustered. "You said something about a nature trail . . ." she managed to get out.

"I guess so." For a crisp corporation lawyer, Scott responded strangely. He stared down at his hands as if surprised to find them still attached and then thrust them in his pockets. "The trail's around here someplace." He took a deep breath and started over. "If you want to see the crater, I'll go back and get my camera."

"Well, whatever you think." As she heard the inanity, Janet's complexion became even more flushed. My lord, she thought, I sound exactly like a recording machine.

If Scott noticed, he was too kind to let on. Apparently he was still having problems of his own. "I'll go back and get it—the camera, I mean." He turned toward the restaurant. "Go ahead and I'll catch up with you in a few minutes. Just follow the signs for Haipu Trail. You can't miss."

"All right." Janet managed to turn and keep from staring at him as he strode back toward Volcano House. Once she had started down the broad track and was safely alone, however, her steps slowed, and she lingered in the middle of a scenic view spot to try and pull herself together before he returned.

She'd *have* to stop behaving like such a cretin! That was all there was to it, she told herself fiercely. The man said one pleasant thing to her and she responded like a lonesome heifer in the springtime. If she kept on in that fashion, she'd make an utter fool of herself before the week was over.

Her gaze swept unhappily over the desert of lava in the crater. Just then her emotions felt as devastated as the barren landscape in front of her. Tangling with Scott had been equal to the force of Madame Pele's eruption . . . or even worse. At least, the elements of nature were now sending up new growth in the twisted fissures of the ruin, but human damage was harder to heal. Deep down, Janet knew that she had been merely marking time, waiting for a man like Scott. To lose him now would destroy her life.

She turned to the path and started down it. She couldn't run away from her thoughts, but if she walked far enough and fast enough—at least the tears would dry on her cheeks before Scott caught up with her.

And for once, she told herself wryly, the surroundings certainly matched her mood. The gray rocks in the crater below were coarse-grained and rough, with jagged, abrasive edges. Around them, the lava flows extended in misshapen, arthritic fingers. Their pockmarked surface was tangible evidence of the fiery temperature during the eruption. The path Janet was on narrowed as it led down into the abyss, clinging to the granite cliff on the right for its support. At times, the trail led behind piles of boulders where tree ferns had sprouted and struggled to maintain life.

About halfway down to the crater, Janet was carefully circumnavigating behind another rocky protrusion when she came upon a fissure on the narrow path ahead of her. She approached it gingerly, peering down to see an eight-foot drop where the sparse soil had washed away. Anyone who missed his step would have a nasty fall onto the rocky cliff, she decided. Then her expression grew more somber as she realized that the short fall could turn into a dangerously long one since the rock sides of the crater were steep and barren of hand-holds. Unless a climber could arrest his descent by finding a fissure on the volcanic face, he'd roll all the way to the bottom.

Janet paused uncertainly in the middle of the path. There was certainly no danger if she took it carefully. Probably she was letting her imagination run riot again; the park rangers would have closed the path if they anticipated any trouble.

She shook her head as if to clear it and approached the break again, allowing plenty of room in case the edges were crumbly. Then, just as she was set to leap across, she suddenly wondered if she should wait for Scott and warn him.

The sound of his voice from the trail above came almost on top of her thoughts.

"Janet . . . where are you?" His cry sliced through the still afternoon air. "Janet! Answer me, for God's sake!"

"I'm down here," she shouted back. "What's the matter?"

He didn't answer her question. Instead, he yelled, "Stay right where you are! Don't move . . . d'ye hear me?"

Alarm sharpened her voice as she dodged a shower of pebbles dislodged by his descent. "Of course I can hear you! What's happened? Are you all right?"

"*I'm* all right . . ." His call sounded more normal now and she caught a glimpse of his figure on the switchback above. Then he emerged from behind the outcropping of boulders with a man in a green uniform a few steps behind.

## THE CAPTURED HEART

"Thank God we caught up with you," Scott managed as he pulled up beside her.

The Hawaiian park ranger wasn't breathing as hard when he came to a stop, but he had a worried expression on his bronzed face. "You shouldn't have come down here, ma'am. This track's been closed to the public ever since that bad rainstorm last week. That's why we put up the barricade. Right past this rock, the whole trail's ready to collapse. We're going to have to rebuild a good part before anybody puts a foot on it."

Janet stood gaping at him, trying to digest his words. "What are you talking about? What barricade?"

"The yellow one that said 'No Trespassing—This path closed until further notice.'" The ranger's tone was as stern as his expression. "We can't make it much plainer for people. It's a good thing I saw your husband start after you. Both of you might have broken your necks. This crater's not the place for rock climbing."

Scott moved restlessly. "If you don't mind . . . let's have the rest of the discussion up on level ground. I'm sure my wife had a good reason . . ."

"You're darned right I did!" Now that her first shock was wearing off, it was being replaced by a more repellent terror. She clutched Scott's arm without realizing it. "There wasn't any barricade on the path. I didn't see anything at all." In the lengthy silence following her remark, she felt Scott's muscle

149

harden under her fingers. "Well, for heaven's sake," her voice rose tremulously, "don't you believe me?"

The park ranger moved then. He turned to Scott and gave him a pitying glance, shaking his head almost imperceptibly.

Janet's eyes widened with alarm. "I wish you'd both stop looking at me as if I'm crazy! I tell you there wasn't any barricade!"

"It's all right, honey." Scott put a protective arm around her shoulders. "Let's go. We'll talk about it later."

"I'm not moving a step until you tell me what's wrong."

His clasp tightened, pulling her close against him, as if he were giving her strength for what was to follow. "There *was* a barricade closing the path—about fifty feet from the start of the trail. Believe me, I'm not mistaken—it was all I could do to shove it aside before I could come looking for you."

## Chapter Seven

Janet opened her eyes the next morning to discover pale bars of sunlight painted across the blanket on the foot of her bed. Her glance moved slowly toward the lanai doors at the end of the room whose slanted louvres provided a preview of the temperature in the world outside. The weather was holding—it was going to be a clear day again.

Then she stirred restlessly as she remembered another sun and another day which had started without a cloud in the sky. Only yesterday, sunbeams had rimmed the fragile profile of a tree fern behind Scott's shoulder on the Haipu Trail. Then she'd learned the truth about the missing barrier, and the fern silhouette had rocked before her eyes like a live thing, before shattering completely as reaction set in.

The interlude of faintness passed, but the shock remained. Scott and the ranger had half-carried her back up the trail, no small feat in itself considering the narrow switchbacks.

Perversely, her frightened reaction had accomplished one thing; at least the ranger had been convinced that her presence on the trail was not a deliberate attempt to thwart park authority. He had been kindness itself in making sure she was safely tucked back in the waiting car. Fortunately, Rodney and the Bristows were already seated on the front seat, and they had started back toward Kaiulani within minutes.

Before Martin and Bonita could mention her white face and dazed manner, Scott had pulled her against his shoulder on the back seat and announced, in a tone that brooked no questions, that she wasn't feeling well. Janet had tried to relax against him, too unhappy to do anything else.

Once they arrived at the hotel, Scott shored her up against his strong body and marched her straight to their room. "Are you able to get out of those clothes by yourself?" he asked brusquely once he had gotten her inside and locked the hall door.

Janet fought against the urge to simply lie down on top of the nearest bed and bury her face in the pillow. She nodded, "I guess so." She watched his tall figure as he bent over his suitcase in the corner of the room. "Scott, do you realize that somebody must have deliberately moved that barrier? I'm not such a fool as to

# THE CAPTURED HEART

lie about a thing like that. They must have wanted me to fall . . . even planned on it."

He straightened and came back to put two white pills on the bed table beside her. "There's no point in talking about it now. Where's your nightgown? I told you to get undressed."

Her fingers went automatically to the buttons of her blouse. "But I *want* to talk about it," she complained to his disappearing back as he headed toward the dressing room. "I tell you—this can't go on. I'm half scared out of my wits. For two cents, I'd get on the next plane for the mainland."

He came back to dump her gown and robe on the bedspread beside her. "For my money, that's what they meant to accomplish. Otherwise you'd have been dead long ago. Here, let me help you with those," he added impatiently, pushing her hand away from the buttons on her cuff. "At this rate, you'll be here for the rest of the night."

"I can manage all right . . ." she began and then fell silent as he simply turned her around and shucked off her blouse and skirt in a stoic, efficient manner. A lacy camisole was dealt with in the same way before he thrust the nightgown in her hands as she stood motionless, clad in a slim petticoat and bra.

The faintest suspicion of amusement crept into his tones. "You'd better take care of the rest yourself. I'd hate to send you into deeper shock." Then, turning toward the bathroom, "I'll get you a glass of water to take those pills. Incidentally, you'd better be in bed when I get back or I'll put you there." He flicked a finger against the nylon in her hand. "Either with or without ruffles."

Janet set a new record in shedding the rest of her clothes, well aware that he meant every word he said. The straps of the green nightgown had barely settled on her shoulders when he reappeared in the open bathroom doorway.

"I *thought* that would get you moving," he said calmly as he came in the room. He watched her get into bed and frowned as he noticed the translucent quality of her complexion. Retrieving the pills from the bed table, he held them out on his open palm. "Swallow these."

"What are they?"

"A mild sedative. Nothing to worry about. A bottle of champagne would achieve the same thing, but then you'd suspect my motives."

"Not yours," she confessed, swallowing the tranquilizers with a sip of water. "But practically everybody else's. If you'd wanted to get rid of me . . ."

"I'd simply have flown back to the mainland in the first place," he finished for her.

"I was going to mention an annulment," she went on as she punched a pillow into shape and leaned back on it. "You're too smart a lawyer to fiddle around with bodies."

"Oh, I agree. Especially with dead ones. No future in it."

She smiled slightly and then sobered as he switched

off the light. "You're not going away now, are you?" she asked. "I know you'll have to eat dinner but you'll be back after that, won't you?"

"I'll be around." His voice sounded rough as he bent over her, but his touch was gentle when he pushed her hair back from her forehead. "Go to sleep now. Everything will look better in the morning."

The old childhood reassurance made her smile wistfully. "How about 'Kiss it and make it well'?"

"Okay, we've nothing to lose." His shoulders blocked the last vestige of twilight from the lanai as he softly kissed her brow.

Surprise left her voice unsteady. "What was that for?"

"I'm covering all bets." He straightened and stood quietly by the bed. "At this point, we can't afford to take any more chances."

Scott's words still seemed to hang in the air as Janet thought about them the next morning. Then she pushed up on an elbow as she heard the sound of a key in their lock and the rattle of dishes from the hallway.

"What on earth . . ." she began as she saw Scott behind the room service cart.

"It's all right," he said. "I intercepted the waiter in the hall. There wasn't any need to waken you but frankly I was starving." He nudged the door closed behind him and paused in the middle of the room. "What's it to be . . . breakfast in bed or the lanai."

She sat up promptly and reached for her robe. "The lanai, please. Otherwise the toast crumbs always end up in the sheets and I manage to butter the blanket."

Scott had been surveying her almost clinically in the dim light but after her comment he chuckled and opened one of the louvred doors. "So be it. I think all that sleep did its work."

Janet finished tying the belt on her robe and stretched luxuriously. "Well, something helped. I feel like a new person."

"You'll feel even better after some coffee. Move, woman." Scott pushed her toward the bath as he leaned over to pick up the remnants of the evening paper which he'd left scattered on the settee. "We'd better evacuate the premises for a discreet interval after breakfast. That maid you were telling me about is hovering in the corridor again. She was upset when I wouldn't let her in the room last night. I guess she thought the world would stop revolving if she didn't turn down the beds. Although she must be used to it by now at this place."

"What do you mean by that?"

His grin was wicked. "This is a honeymoon hotel. The guests have other things on their minds. Maybe that's why the management hired a maid who doesn't speak English. They *know* she'll be discreet."

She smiled in response. "I hardly think Kaiulani would stoop that low. Besides Wayne insisted that all their help did speak English."

Scott looked up from transferring napkins to the table. "That reminds me—Marshall called last night after you'd gone to sleep."

Janet's hand went up to her lips. "I'd forgotten all about him. Remember—Rodney said he was looking for me yesterday. What did he want?"

"To say that some of the choicer Exhibit pieces have arrived. He thought you'd like to watch the uncrating today." Scott reached for his glass of juice and took a swallow. "I told him it was out of the question."

"You did *what?*"

"Whatever your other failings, you're not deaf," he informed her austerely. "I thought you were going to get ready for breakfast."

Janet waved that aside. "But how could you tell Wayne that? Checking the Exhibit is part of my job. Judge Byrne will never forgive me."

"After yesterday, you're in no condition to stand around opening packing crates, and if you don't have sense enough to know it, then it's time somebody made up your mind for you."

"But you had no right . . ." she began only to fall silent as his jaw firmed. Finally, she tried another tack. "Maybe if I just looked on for a few minutes . . ."

Scott tested the side of the coffee pot with the back of his hand. "You'd get farther trying to convince me if you did your arguing *after* breakfast. This coffee's getting cold."

After that, peace lasted through the meal on the

sunny terrace. From time to time, Janet noticed Scott watching her from under hooded lids, as if he weren't quite sure what her next move was going to be. She was still trying to decide herself when the telephone rang sharply and brought her halfway to her feet.

"Sit down . . . I'll get it," Scott informed her, shoving back his chair. He was through the louvred doors and over to the bedroom table before Janet could protest.

"Hello—" Scott's terse tone should have discouraged even the most determined telephone solicitor, Janet decided. But evidently it didn't have the desired effect. She saw his lips tighten before saying, "Yes, Martin . . . I recognized your voice. Nice of you to call." There was a considerable pause. Then, "She's feeling better, thanks, but I'm keeping her under wraps today just the same. Nothing more strenuous than lolling on the beach. Let us have a raincheck on your offer, will you?" Martin's reply brought a frown to his face. "Yes, that's what I understand from Marshall. A few of the exhibits have arrived. No, he didn't say which ones . . . you'll have to ask him." There was another pause which Scott evidently made no attempt to break. Finally, he said briskly, "Well, thanks again for calling . . . I'll tell Janet you sent your best. So long."

He replaced the receiver and stood looking down at it for a moment before rejoining her on the lanai. "You heard?"

"The Bristows . . ."

"Send their best. Or, at least, Martin does. Bonita had gone to the hairdresser's, but she wanted us to join them later. They've hired a boat for the day."

"I gather we're not accepting . . ." Her tone was dry.

"Go to the head of the class. After yesterday, you'll have to explain if you wander farther than the hall door. The Bristows are definitely off-limits."

"Because they knew I was on that path?"

Scott's lips settled in a grim line. "Something like that. The police in Hilo have sent another query about Martin to the mainland as well as adding extra security for the Exhibit. That display's going to be so airtight when it's finally opened that it will be difficult to even breathe. And once the thing is underway, my girl"— he pointed a finger for emphasis—"we're getting out. Straight back to the mainland."

Janet stared at him with astonished eyes, uncertain what to reply. From the determined tone of his voice, it wasn't the time to start raising feeble objections and for some reason that seemed to be all she was capable of these days.

"Better get changed and we'll go down on the beach." Scott was looking at his watch again as he turned toward the dressing room. "I'll be ready in a couple of shakes and then the place is all yours."

Janet protested mildly, "I don't know how I managed before you appeared. All week you've been telling me when to eat and when to sleep and when to brush my teeth."

He grinned at her unrepentantly. "Tooth brushing comes first—then you get in a swimsuit. I just explained. Next time pay attention." His expression sobered. "I hope that pool episode didn't discourage you."

"Of course not." She surveyed her fingertips carefully. "Whatever your faults, I don't think you plan to shove me under a wave."

"Careful . . . you'll turn my head."

"Umm." She moved over to the telephone. "I'll call Wayne Marshall and tell him I'll be back at work tomorrow. Although what he's going to think when I goof off today . . ."

"He'll think that you're behaving like a typical female guest at Kaiulani—getting a tan on the beach with her husband."

"That's hardly an apt description . . . we're scarcely a typical couple."

"Why?" His eyebrows went up. "For all intents and purposes we certainly are. If you want the game as well as the name, all you have to do is change the ground rules."

"Don't be insulting."

Unexpectedly, he broke out laughing. "Honey, I don't know where you've been all these years. Most women wouldn't call that an insult." He moved on into the bathroom. "I'll get ready while you're phoning. Don't let Marshall try to change your mind."

Wayne Marshall didn't. Evidently he had taken Scott's warning seriously. "After all, there's no reason

# THE CAPTURED HEART

for you to concern yourself with actually setting up the Exhibit," he said when she started apologizing. "We have so many plainclothesmen stacked up in the corners of the room already that there's hardly any space left."

"That sounds ominous. Anything special happened lately?"

"As if you didn't know." Wayne's voice was aggrieved. "From what I hear, you go from one cliffhanger to another. That husband of yours is pretty upset about it."

Janet frowned at the receiver. "You mean that's why you have all the extra security men?" she asked finally.

"Not exactly—but you're a contributing factor. Actually we've just received notice of an added attraction they've sent for the Exhibit. It's an eighteenth-century wooden horse from Japan complete with saddle and trappings of gold and precious jewels."

"Not life-size, surely?"

"No—only three feet high but worth a king's ransom and I've spent the last hour on the phone determining that we're properly insured."

"It sounds fabulous," Janet enthused. "I can't wait to see it."

"No dice. From the way that husband of yours talked, he'd demand a raincheck for you if a miracle was scheduled. The horse can wait."

"If you say so . . ."

"I'm just seconding the motion because I know

what's good for me. Sometime you'll have to tell me what women see in these masterful men." His voice turned brisk. "Right now I'd better get back to work."

"I'll let you go, then," she told him hastily as she heard the bathroom door open behind her.

Wayne's chuckle came over the wire. "You're going to have to stop jumping every time he comes in the room."

"How did you know?"

"Your voice is a dead giveaway. I'm beginning to think there's a place for the mere male in this world, after all."

"I'll talk to you later," she said severely.

Wayne was chuckling as he rang off. "I'll be here."

Janet turned to find Scott, in swim trunks and a matching shirt, rummaging through some papers on the desk. "It would be nice to know what you told Wayne," she complained. "He seems to have some strange ideas about things."

Scott dismissed her with a cursory glance before turning his attention to the desk top again. "I can't remember anything earthshaking but if you want a philosophical discussion, we can hold it on the beach. Providing we ever get there."

"I'm going to change now," she snapped, moving over to do just that.

"Good. I hoped you might."

"And I have no intention of a philosophical discussion . . ."

"Better still." He found the paper he wanted and slid it into an envelope before turning to face her. "Earthshaking theories don't go with hot dogs. You end up with indigestion every time."

She was interested despite herself. "How did hot dogs get into this?"

"That's what we're having for lunch. They sell them under that cluster of heliotrope trees down by the water. If you're good, I might buy you a cold beer, too."

She wrinkled her nose. "Big deal. I've had better offers."

"No doubt. But not this morning." He checked his watch. "And unless you're in a swimsuit pretty damned fast, I'll trade you in on an excursion to go fishing."

When they finally stretched out on the white sand beach a little later, Scott didn't appear to be suffering from marlin or barracuda withdrawal symptoms. He relaxed on an oversized beach towel, muttered, "This is the life," and promptly closed his eyes.

Janet waited a little longer before following suit. She adjusted a pair of sunglasses to diffuse the glare from the brilliant white sand, noting the gentle foaming breakers on the curve of the bay for future reference before stretching out on her own towel. She tried to ignore Scott's tanned forearm alongside hers and forced herself to concentrate on the palm trees which edged the beach like graceful sentinels. Then as the marvelous warmth of the sun started soaking into her body, she let her tense muscles relax.

The next thing she felt was a firm hand on her thigh. "Damned if you don't need a keeper." Scott was sitting up, frowning at her. "A few more minutes of that sun and you'll be in trouble. I thought redheads had more sense . . ."

Groggily she sat up beside him. "What's the matter . . . how long has it been?" She tested the skin on the bridge of her nose and winced.

"That's what I mean." Scott hauled her erect and jerked his head toward some shaded sand under the palms, while he scooped up their towels. "You have to get used to this sun. I found out the hard way when I was fishing off Kona."

Janet was checking the clock on a nearby cabana. "There's no harm done. I may peel a little, but it won't be a catastrophe." She helped him lay out the towels again before sitting down on one, tailor-fashion. "I'm more in danger of collapsing from malnutrition. You *did* say something about hot dogs?"

He glanced at her in pretended amazement. "You *can't* be hungry already. We just finished breakfast a little while ago."

"Try me." She jerked her head toward the refreshment stand down the beach. "The smell of those hot dogs is devastating."

"And I thought you were the truffles-and-champagne type."

"That will teach you to generalize. Women don't fit into neat little categories." Then she adjusted her

## THE CAPTURED HEART

sunglasses as a sturdy figure came hurrying toward them. "Isn't that Thelma Kahori?"

"Looks like it. She seems worried, too. I wonder what's up." His eyebrows drew together for a second before he drawled, "She probably wants to talk to you. I'll go get our lunch. Remember, though, you're staying put."

"Yes, master." She made a face at him. "Is it all right to quiver a little if Robert Redford walks by?"

He just grinned and put on his shirt. "Two hot dogs coming up."

Janet's features sobered as she turned to see Thelma hovering uncertainly on the path behind her. The older woman was carrying a wide, shallow basket of flowers, but it was her solemn expression which brought Janet to her feet. "Why, Mrs. Kahori . . . is something wrong?"

"I . . . I hope not." The hostess fingered the rattan basket handle nervously. "Have you seen Rodney this morning, Mrs. Frazier?"

"No . . . but then I really haven't seen anybody." Janet moved over beside her. "We came right down here after leaving our room. Why? Is Rodney missing?"

"Not in the way you mean." Thelma managed to smile although her eyes were still troubled. "He and his wife had a disagreement this morning. Over money again. I guess he left the apartment in a temper. These young people . . ." She sighed and shook her head. "They have so much to learn."

165

"Don't we all," Janet murmured.

The older woman nodded. "I thought if I saw him before my class, I'd ask him to call home. This is no time for him to be upsetting his wife."

"I'm sure he'll turn up." Janet sought a change of subject. "Are your flowers for something special?"

"My lei class . . . some guests like to try their hand at it. Why don't you come along?"

"I'd like to," Janet said truthfully, eyeing the contents of the basket with interest. "What kind of flowers are you using?"

"Orchids, two kinds of Crown flowers . . . both the purple and white . . . and red ginger leaves for contrast." She patted a case at the side of the basket. "This holds the lei needles and heavy thread."

"It sounds like fun, but I'm grounded for the rest of today. My husband," she explained when Thelma looked mystified. "He's decided we're spending the day on the beach." And then she bit the edge of her lip in bemusement when she realized that she'd made the statement like a wife of years' standing.

Thelma evidently saw nothing amiss. "You might as well enjoy this good weather now because I heard on the radio that there's a storm front moving in. But don't forget our tour of the hotel before you get busy with the Exhibit."

"It's at the top of my list. I hope you find Rodney soon," Janet added as the hostess started to move off.

"Oh, he'll turn up." There was an undercurrent of resignation in the other's voice. "He needs me these

## THE CAPTURED HEART

days almost more than I need him. Enjoy yourself, Mrs. Frazier."

"Thank you, I will." Janet stared after her with a puzzled expression.

"What was on the old girl's mind?" Scott's voice sounded behind Janet's shoulder.

She turned to find him balancing a paper plate full of food with one hand and carrying two bottles of beer in the other. "Nothing . . . really. Let me help you with those."

"Take the plate with the hot dogs. I'll hold the beer until you get settled."

"You don't approve of adding sand for flavor?" she teased, lowering herself carefully onto the towel.

"Only for canaries. I hope you wanted mustard on your hot dog." He sat down beside her and anchored the beer bottles firmly between them.

"Would it do any good to say no?"

"Not the slightest." He was handing her a napkin which had been stuffed in his shirt pocket as an obvious afterthought. Then he frowned as he looked across at her. "You're not serious, are you?"

"Certainly not." Janet helped herself to a still-steaming hot dog. "The more mustard the better."

"Good." The word was muffled as Scott took a satisfied bite. "You were going to tell me about Thelma."

"She was just looking for Rodney. Trying to smooth over a family fight between him and her daughter-in-law."

"I thought she had more sense." Scott stared idly

up the path where the older woman had disappeared. "Evidently the maid wasn't involved . . ."

"What maid?"

"Ours. They were huddled in the doorway after Thelma left you. I wonder when that girl gets around to making any beds."

Janet blotted her lips with the napkin and took a sip of beer before answering. "Darned if I know. She seems to work the strangest schedule . . . from early morning to late at night. It must be a split shift."

"Beats me how the hotel can get away with it. I suppose a job at Kaiulani is worth some inconvenience, though."

"Thelma did say that most of their employees stayed for years."

Scott finished his last bite and leaned back on his elbows as he noted the peaceful scene in front of him. "Can't say I blame them. Most people would give their shirts for even two weeks of this."

From his casual tone, it was hard to decide whether he meant the tranquility of the sunswept beach or whether he was talking about their new life together.

For a lawyer, Janet thought with some vexation, he was amazingly inarticulate. At the same time, she was distressingly aware of why she wanted him to be more specific.

"You're very quiet suddenly." Scott had turned and was staring at her. "For a minute, you looked as if you were a million miles away."

"Hardly. You're imagining things," she parried,

wishing that she could stop the verbal fencing and tell the truth for a change. Then, she reminded herself grimly that the truth would send her new husband flying in the opposite direction. Scott Frazier was not a man to welcome domestic curbs; he'd made that more than evident. Just because he'd been conscientious lately didn't mean that he was signing any long-term contracts.

"The hell I am. Maybe you were in the sun too long." His tone became concerned. "What's the matter . . . don't you feel well? You haven't finished your hot dog."

"I'm fine," she insisted stubbornly, wishing that he'd stop probing. "What's on the schedule for this afternoon?"

"I suppose I should get some work done. There's nothing that I can't finish in the room, but it won't be very thrilling for you."

Janet couldn't very well tell him that just having him around was quite enough. She appeared to be losing her powers of speech as well as her appetite.

"Was there anything special you wanted to do?" Scott was asking. "And don't mention that damned Exhibit . . ."

"I had no intention of it." She brushed some sand from her knee. "Since I'm not going to earn my salary, I'll vegetate on the lanai with a book."

"Then make sure you stay in the shade."

"You're doing it again," she reminded him softly.

"Doing what?"

"Telling me what to do."

"Relax, honey," his tone was offhand. "You might as well get used to it."

The rest of the day passed in the same low-key atmosphere. Janet was amazed to find how pleasant it was to sprawl on the lounge on their lanai and read her book. From time to time, when her thoughts wandered from the printed page, she'd simply close her eyes and enjoy the soft, plumeria-scented air, content to savor what she had and stop trying to forecast future events.

Twilight was descending fast when she heard Scott bundling his work into his attaché case. He turned off the desk lamp before getting up, stretching lengthily, and making his way to the door of the lanai.

His glance at her was apprehensive, "So much for hitching your fate to a busy lawyer. Did you think I'd deserted you forever?"

Janet shook her head and stood up. "Not at all. I knew you were busy."

His features relaxed in a weary grin. "Well, you certainly deserve a reward for being so patient. Put on your best bib and tucker and let's investigate the dining room."

She pretended surprise. "No more hot dogs?"

"Not tonight. But don't think this sets a pattern for the future."

Janet kept her voice light as she brushed by him. "Wouldn't dream of it. You mean really dressed up?"

"For you, I'll dust off a black tie. What time shall I

make reservations? Three quarters of an hour? Or can a woman get ready in that time?"

"This one can," she said and closed the bathroom door decisively behind her.

Janet's first sight of the hotel's main dining room made her draw in her breath with delight. It was constructed on multilevels with long windows overlooking the floodlit beach. Natural cork tiles formed the walls and lined the ceiling between exposed teak beams. Patches of color came from the lavish flower arrangements which separated the dining levels; bouquets of dark red ginger, scarlet anthurium, and exotic bird-of-paradise blooms to make the room a tropical solarium. The tables were equally eye-catching with orange lacquer serving plates atop dark brown cloths and squat russet candles in brass bases.

A smiling hostess with a spray of plumeria blossoms tucked in her black hair led them down to a corner window table. She presented them with outsized menus and murmured, "Enjoy your dinner," before gliding off.

It was hard to do anything else, Janet decided later after successive courses of Alaska Crab Legs Ravigote, Asparagus Soup, Filet Mignon topped with a Medallion of Fois Gras de Strasbourg, and a succulent wedge of Sacher Torte.

"I have never . . . ever . . . eaten such food," she confessed when black coffee was finally poured and Scott reached for a cigarette. "The only thing that could qualify for a finishing touch would be a handmaiden peeling grapes after I've staggered onto a couch."

He grinned. "It makes a change from hot dogs. I'm glad to see that you've recovered your appetite."

"After that dinner, I'll have to lose it again for the rest of the week. Now I understand why all the women around here wear muu-muus. They probably haven't seen their waistlines in years."

"You don't have to worry." His glance went deliberately over her dress of sparkly platinum. "And you can skip the muu-muus—you're doing just fine the way things are." Catching sight of an advancing waiter carrying a plug-in telephone, he frowned. "Damn it all—*now* what?"

"The price of fame," she murmured mischievously. "Nobody ever calls me on the telephone at dinner."

"Mr. Frazier?" The waiter's question took Scott's attention but not before he'd raised a warning eyebrow at her impudence. "Sorry to bother you, sir . . ." the young man was plugging the cord in a convenient baseboard outlet after putting the telephone at Scott's elbow. "They mentioned it was important."

"Thanks." Scott picked up the receiver to say, "Frazier . . . oh, hello, Tom," and then frowned in concentration as he listened to the voice at his ear.

From his brief monosyllabic replies in the next minute or two, Janet deduced "Tom" was an important rancher-client who believed that attorneys should be on call at his convenience.

"Tonight?" Scott was asking in a pained tone.

"Wouldn't tomorrow do as well? After all, there's no great rush." He scowled again at the argument his remark brought forth before admitting. "Well, if you're flying to Honolulu tonight, I suppose we'd better get it clarified. Where are you now . . . at home or the airport?" He listened for a minute and his expression lightened. "I'd appreciate your stopping by the hotel if you can. We didn't have anything special planned and this shouldn't take long." His look across the table was an unspoken question and Janet nodded reassuringly. "Okay, Tom," he said into the receiver again. "Fifteen minutes from now in the lobby. I'll have the papers ready. See you."

Janet watched him hang up and lean back so the waiter, who had been hovering discreetly nearby, could unplug the phone and take it away.

"So much for our undisturbed evening," Scott told Janet ruefully. He signaled for the check, and signed it with a brevity of motion that characterized most of his movements. "I'm sorry about this," he went on, "but Tom shouts too loud to be ignored. Actually, this business shouldn't take long if you don't mind being parked in a corner for a while."

"It doesn't matter a bit." Janet reached for her stole and pulled it around her shoulders while he stubbed out his cigarette. He stood up and moved the table so that she could get out easily before following her up the shallow steps to the dining room entrance.

"I have to go back to the room and get those papers

I was talking about. Want to come along?" he asked as they moved on to the lower lobby level.

"It's such a pretty night, I'd rather window-shop if you don't mind." She indicated the brightly lit display windows of Kaiulani's gift shop and apparel boutique whose doors were still invitingly open. "I promise faithfully to stay away from the exhibit area upstairs."

He grinned. "It's locked anyhow with a guard at every door."

"Then I can't get in any trouble. And you don't have to worry about any lurking strangers. This part of the hotel is like Times Square."

"Okay." Scott glanced at his watch and decided not to argue. "Shopping sounds harmless enough. How about meeting me in the lobby in a half hour or so. We should be finished with business by then and I'd like to have Tom meet you."

"All right." She decided his sudden mellowness must be the result of dinner. Maybe it was true that an ounce of filet mignon went further than the same amount of French perfume. As he still lingered beside her, she said, "You'd better get going or your client will be tearing the roof off the place."

"All right." He sounded reluctant. "Don't forget your itinerary . . . shopping and then the lobby."

She started to laugh. "I don't need a road map. Go *on*."

He shook his head and strode off. Janet watched him until he vaulted up the shallow stone steps two at

## THE CAPTURED HEART

a time and then turned to the serious business of inspecting the boutique windows.

Thelma found her there, debating whether to buy a lilac polka-dot blouse when she strolled through a few minutes later.

"Most of our women guests stand here sooner or later," she teased, drawing up beside her. "I'm amazed you've resisted this long."

Janet turned in surprise and then smiled. "You're just in time to tell me that I need a polka-dot blouse like an extra arm."

Thelma shook her head. "No, ma'am. Not with that blouse and that hair of yours. The color combination would be sensational!"

Janet suddenly noticed a discreetly placed price tag hanging from the sleeve of the blouse and shook her head. "Get thee behind me . . ." she said, moving purposefully away. "Aren't you working late?" she asked conversationally as Thelma walked beside her.

"A little. Some of the help have been sick so we've had to double up." The older woman went on hurriedly as if she wanted to change the subject. "I didn't expect to see you by yourself at this time of night. Is Mr. Frazier working again?"

"Not for long." Janet wondered for a moment how Scott's activities had come to be common knowledge and then forgot about it as an idea presented itself. "This would be a fine time for me to tour behind the scenes if you could manage it. Scott's going to be busy for a half hour or so."

Glenna Finley

Thelma looked at her watch and came to a decision. "I don't see why not," she allowed. "Mr. Marshall wanted you to have an idea of how the hotel functioned. A few of the departments are closed now, but most of them are open 'round the clock.' We'll turn in here." She stopped in front of an inconspicuous door at the end of the arcade corridor. "You probably didn't realize it but there are duplicate corridors throughout the building . . . one set for employees and another for guests." She motioned for Janet to follow her down the new hallway to emphasize her point.

The staff service corridor was brightly lit and lined with maintenance equipment in orderly storage. A long line of baggage carts were stacked close by, making Janet recall that she hadn't seen one in evidence since the porter had delivered her luggage.

"We want our guests to find complete tranquility in their part of the hotel," Thelma went on. "Even the room maids are ordered to store their linen carts in these corridors if they can."

"The one who does our room must have gotten her instructions confused," Janet said with a smile. "But now that I think of it—her cart is the only one I've seen out in the hall."

"That girl has trouble remembering some things," Thelma sighed and gestured into a room they were passing. "This is where our florist does her work."

Rows of vases lined the walls of the room except for one side where a big glass-fronted refrigerator re-

## THE CAPTURED HEART

vealed shelves full of leis and buckets of cut flowers.

"No wonder this place looks like a greenhouse," Janet said appreciatively.

"Hilo is the orchid capital of the world, so we don't have to go far for our materials. And, of course, the hotel gardeners supply plumeria and the bird-of-paradise blooms." Thelma moved on down the corridor, pointing out other immaculate maintenance rooms on either side.

When they had passed the main kitchens with their hordes of cooks and waiters, they came upon the pastry department where two jovial chefs insisted they sample some cookies just out of the oven.

"I shouldn't have weakened," Janet told Thelma when they finally broke away and were touring the employees' cafeteria. "After that piece of Sacher Torte I finished at dinner, I planned to skip eating for a week."

"You won Karl's heart when you praised his cookies. He's from Vienna and convinced that Austrian pastry beats every other kind," Thelma said genially. "You'll probably have an extra plate of sweet rolls delivered to your door in the morning."

"That's a worse temptation than the polka-dot blouse." Janet stopped outside the housekeeping department and stared into a storage room of neatly stacked linen. "Honestly, this is the most fantastically organized hotel I've ever seen. It's no wonder you've won an international reputation."

"It's all in our day's work," Thelma said calmly

but her face showed how pleased she was by the compliment. "Actually, I think you've seen—" Suddenly she stopped in the middle of her sentence and stared over Janet's shoulder with a stricken look. "Hana, what are you doing here?"

Janet turned to see a young Eurasian girl who looked very pregnant despite the camouflage of her turquoise muu-muu hurrying toward them.

"I had to come, Thelma. Rod wouldn't pay any attention to me . . . he said it was too late now to change his plans . . ." Belatedly she took in Janet's quiet figure in the doorway and sent a beseeching glance toward the older woman. "I'm . . . I'm sorry," she faltered. "I didn't realize you were busy."

"Mrs. Frazier, this is my daughter-in-law, Hana," Thelma muttered, obviously distressed by what the girl had said. "If you'd excuse us a minute or two . . ."

"Of course." Janet looked around for a place to melt into the background and discovered the linen room offered the only possibility. "I'll wait in here unless the housekeeper would object . . ."

"No, of course not." The preoccupied look on Thelma's face showed that she had already dismissed her from her mind. She was drawing Rodney's wife over to the other side of the hallway. "Hana . . . are you sure? Did you tell him what I said, too?"

"I told him everything I could think of." In her agitation, Hana's voice carried clearly. "He said this was our only chance to make any decent money . . . that we needed it to pay the bills. I told him he was crazy.

# THE CAPTURED HEART

He'll be caught eventually, Thelma—then what will I do?" She covered her face with her hands and started to sob.

"Hush, girl. Crying won't help." Thelma pulled her against her broad bosom and rocked her as she would a child. "We'll have to find a way to stop him."

"I hitched a ride here. If I could find one of the men quitting work, maybe I could get a lift and go after Rod . . ."

"You know what the obstetrician told you!" Thelma's voice was a whiplash. "It was a fool thing for you to come this far."

"But I had to let you know." Hana raised her head and stared defiantly through wet lashes.

"*Auwe!* If I only knew how to drive . . ." Thelma looked around abstractedly as if hoping to find a solution to the dilemma within sight.

Janet felt the hostess's gaze land on her and stared nervously back. "If there's anything I could do to help," she offered, "I'll be glad to."

"Do you drive, Mrs. Frazier?"

Janet advanced to the doorway. "Well, yes . . . but I don't have a car. Unless Scott's rental one is still around somewhere."

Thelma cut her off with a brisk gesture. "Mr. Marshall has a business car in the lot. I know where he keeps the key."

"But you'd have to ask him . . ." Janet found herself trailing in the wake of the Hawaiian woman who was pulling Hana along at her side.

"He's too busy with the Exhibit to want to be bothered. Tonight he's entertaining some members of the Japanese consulate. Besides, the fewer people who know about this . . . the better. Rodney needs his job here."

"I'm sure Wayne would be discreet," Janet protested as Thelma moved out of the employees' corridor and into the business offices of the hotel behind the main desk. "It would only take a minute . . ."

"I can tell him after you're on the way." Thelma reached in the top drawer of a file cabinet and pulled a key ring from a cigar box at the front of it. "I *knew* he kept an extra set of car keys here," she exclaimed triumphantly. "Hana . . . you wait in my office until I come back. You should be off your feet. I suppose Rodney was going to Wainani?"

Hana nodded unhappily.

"Did he say what time he was meeting the plane?" Thelma asked. "There's no point in all this if Mrs. Frazier can't head him off."

"It's all right." Hana's voice sounded as if she wasn't far from exhaustion. "He said the pilot didn't like the weather report, so there's still another hour before the pickup."

"I don't understand what this is all about. You can't expect me to do something blindfolded—" Janet began when Thelma cut her off.

"There just isn't time to explain it now, Mrs. Frazier. You heard Hana. It will take you over forty minutes to reach the airfield if you leave now."

# THE CAPTURED HEART

"An airfield by Wainani Bay?" Janet persisted.

"That's right. It's on the northern coast of the island. I can give you directions on how to find it."

"You're in luck . . . I've been there."

"At the airport?" The older woman's face turned watchful as Hana gave a frightened gasp behind them.

"No, I just saw the signpost to the airport. Look, what *is* all this? From what I remember, that airport was abandoned."

Thelma shook her head. "It's used occasionally. Hana, you wait on the couch here! After I put Mrs. Frazier in the car, I'll take you to my room so you can get your feet up." Without waiting for a response, she urged Janet out into the hall.

"I'll have to tell my husband I'm going," Janet decided aloud before they came to the big glass doors of the entrance. "He should be here in the lobby talking to a client." Anxiously, she scanned the room, looking for Scott's figure on one of the scattered divans.

"I don't see him anywhere," Thelma put in. "You're sure he didn't mean the lower lobby?"

"I didn't think so." She turned to Thelma. "And I can't just go wandering off. He'd be furious."

"If that's all it is, there's no need to worry." The other woman patted her wrist comfortingly. "I promise to tell him where you've gone before he has a chance to worry. I give you my word, Mrs. Frazier." Her gaze was steady as it held Janet's. "Don't forget,

181

I'm trusting you with my son's safety, and Hana has to trust both of us."

"Well, if you put it that way—there's not much I can say."

"Then you'd better get started." Thelma swept her through the entrance doors, ignoring the greeting of the doorman by the curb as she marched Janet along the curving drive. She paused beside a dark sedan parked halfway down. "This is Mr. Marshall's car," she said, unlocking the door and then thrusting the key into Janet's hand. "I'll explain to him, too."

The younger woman slid gingerly onto the front seat. "I certainly hope so. Otherwise, I can see myself trying to explain a stolen car to one of your highway patrolmen." Her eyebrows drew together. "On second thought, you'd better tell Wayne about the car *before* you bother looking for my husband."

"I've *told* you, I'll take care of all that." Thelma's impatience was evident despite her controlled tone. "Remember, you stay on the main highway north until you're about five miles from Mahukona. There isn't a sign for the turn-off but there's a grocery store and lunch counter place about a half mile before you come to the intersection. After that . . ."

"I drive down almost to the water where there's a fork in the road, leading to the airport," Janet said. "I remember."

"Then you *were* at the airport."

"No. We stayed on the other fork which went down through the cane fields to the beach. It was a picnic—"

## THE CAPTURED HEART

She broke off hurriedly. "Not that it matters now. The important thing is—what do I tell Rodney once I get to the airfield?"

"Tell him that Hana needs him and that I . . ." Thelma's voice faltered and then gained strength, "that I *insist* he come back. Before he gets involved any further. Tell him I've found another way." The hostess closed the car door and stood there impassively as Janet rolled down the driver's window for a final plea.

"It would carry a lot more weight with Rodney if you told him in person," she urged. "Can't you come along?"

"It's better if I'm not there. My son will understand. You'd better go now, Mrs. Frazier."

Her calm dictate held such authority that Janet obediently pulled away from the curb.

She turned left at the junction and accelerated toward the main road marked "Mahukona—north" while she thought about Thelma's last comment.

Why her presence would carry more weight with Rodney than his mother, she couldn't imagine. Unless there was someone that Thelma didn't want to meet at the abandoned airport.

Janet's fingers tightened on the steering wheel as that possibility occurred to her. Then she shook her head as if to clear it and pressed down harder on the accelerator when the new highway showed straight and clear in front of her.

All she had to do was deliver the message, she told

herself firmly. There was no reason to let her imagiation run riot in the process. Rodney was a nice young man who was evidently using the wrong tactics to earn some money. It wasn't surprising that his wife and mother wanted to stop him. Even Scott wouldn't find anything wrong in that.

The sudden mental vision of Scott made her peer worriedly through the windshield. Surely Thelma could be trusted to tell him where she'd gone. Even if she didn't volunteer the information, the doorman had seen them beside Wayne's car. All Scott had to do was ask.

Janet's lips curved in a rueful smile. At least she had no doubt that Scott *would* ask. Afterwards, she'd have to explain this drive in great detail to avoid another dressing-down. As she reached forward to turn on the car radio and find some music, she acknowledged that his concern was the most reassuring thing about this whole escapade.

At the roadside, the reflection of her headlights caught the tall stands of Australian Pine or Ironwood trees whose tufted needles looked like lacy paper cutouts against the landscape. Overhead, the moon slipped through scattered cloud cover as the miles passed on the drive north. At times the deserted landscape was bathed in its platinum rays. Then darkness would descend abruptly as the clouds made their next move. Eventually the brisk wind which was bending the roadside stands of wild cane would send the clouds on their way and start the cycle all over again.

# THE CAPTURED HEART

By the time Janet reached the turn-off that Thelma had mentioned, the moon was making a triumphant return and the dingy outlines of the neighborhood grocery and lunch counter were clearly visible. Window displays advertising "Kalua Pork" and "Homemade Poi" stood out starkly as well as a poorly lettered "Closed" sign hanging from the shade on the lunch counter door.

"Not exactly like Hollywood and Vine," Janet murmured over the program of Japanese music which the local disk jockeys seemed to prefer. She signaled for the left turn across the highway and slowed as the car left the hard-surfaced highway for the dirt track leading to Wainani Bay.

If she had been in doubt as to her directions, an old airport sign on the shoulder of the road would have reassured her.

Other than that marker, there was little to comfort her on any other score. The tall cane fields on both sides of the car made her feel as if she were following a shadowed swath through the wilderness. When she and Scott had come that way, the sunshine and brilliant blue sky had caught her attention. Now the clouds had thickened and the six-foot cane fronds looked like accusing fingers as they bent toward the car.

Janet swallowed and took a deep breath. This was no time for girlish tremors, she told herself silently. It was an effort not to say it aloud. Anything to break the thick stillness that descended on the car after she'd clicked off the program of Oriental music which grated like fingernails on a slate blackboard in her prejudiced ears.

Her headlights dipped abruptly as her front wheels jolted through a series of potholes. She tightened her grip on the steering wheel nervously to compensate. "Slow down and be careful!" she told herself fiercely, knowing a broken axle would be catastrophic. God knows how long she'd have to sit at the roadside before help came along.

Although surely Rodney would see her plight when he returned to Kaiulani. That thought offered such possibilities that she almost let the car slip beyond the gravel shoulder. She pulled back to the crown of the road quickly and then went on wondering.

Nobody had hazarded a guess as to Rodney's future plans. He was just supposed to stop what he was doing. Beyond that, his career loomed as murky as the clouds overhead.

Janet tried to consider it dispassionately. She was simply there to deliver a message, she told herself. If Rodney needed a keeper—as he seemed to—then Hana and Thelma could take turns applying for the job.

It was a relief to vent her annoyance on Rodney's absent figure and try to smother the nigglings of fear which had grown monstrously ever since she'd turned off the highway. If only she'd remembered how isolated this damned road was! Or if she'd stopped to think that an abandoned airport was even *more* isolated. Then she could have confessed that she wasn't the type for such goings-on, and Thelma would have recruited another messenger for her particular Garcia.

Some of Scott's more scathing comments on her past ability to take care of herself came back into her mind like a haunting melody. Defiantly she reached over to turn the radio on again, preferring even the discord of Oriental music to the particular refrain she was harboring.

The fork to the airport loomed up a minute or two later and she turned on a track which deteriorated with every foot of the way. The car jounced through the rough and rocky surface like a demonstration model for a television tire commercial. Janet hung on grimly and hoped that Wayne Marshall wouldn't sue when he saw his undercarriage the next day.

Then, abruptly, the road ended at a sagging barbed-wire fence which rimmed the airfield. Janet barely had time to brake and park alongside a battered pickup truck, letting the motor idle as she leaned through her open window to peer at the dark interior of the pickup's cab. If Rodney had been there, he had gone on to other places. Reluctantly she cut the ignition and seconds later switched off her headlights.

The moon picked that moment to duck behind a thick cloud and stay there. "Damn!" Janet said, staring out at the gloom, and then said, "Damn!" again with considerable feeling. When that didn't help, she rummaged for a flashlight in the glove compartment to improve matters. If she didn't find one, she'd start the car again, lean on the horn, and give Rodney about thirty seconds to appear.

When her fingers closed around the familiar metal shape, she knew that her defiant decision had just been altered. Now she wouldn't have any excuse for avoiding a walk over to the ramshackle structure at the end of the runway or even to the beach beyond. She had promised Thelma; the fact that her backbone had lost all its stiffening didn't compensate for breaking her word.

She got out of the car and closed the door quietly, strangely reluctant to break the stillness of the night. Turning on the flashlight beam, she picked her way carefully across to the fence. She pulled apart the sagging barbed wires and crawled through onto the grass landing strip. Her shoes made soft, slithering sounds as she crossed the dry turf. Otherwise she could only hear the pounding of the breakers on the rocky shore beyond.

The shadowed outlines of the deserted building loomed up in front of her. She stopped and flashed the beam of her light over the structure. A tattered wind-sock flew from the top of the roof above two gaping holes that showed in place of windows and a door that leaned precariously inward from one hinge. Inside, she could see the remnants of a counter and a chair with a broken back; everything else had been removed long ago.

## THE CAPTURED HEART

Then, as the moon emerged to illuminate the landscape, she flicked off her flashlight and turned to survey the deserted airstrip again. The short grass on the runway bent in a sudden gust of wind and a loose board hanging at the side of the building behind her creaked in protest.

The noise made her start with nervousness. There was no reason for her panic; there wasn't a human being in sight. Hana had either gotten her times wrong or Rodney had changed the rendezvous. All that was left for her to do now was to return to Kaiulani and report that she'd missed him.

Janet started back the way she'd come. At least she could truthfully say that Rodney's plans were poorly conceived. No pilot was going to attempt a night landing on that strip in its current state. Not if he wanted to live to talk about it.

Carefully she pulled apart the strands of wire on the fence and stepped through them again, happy that she managed without snagging a stocking or catching the skirt of her dress. She looked down at her satin evening pumps and started to giggle. Of all the ridiculous outfits to be negotiating barbed-wire fences!

"Something funny, Mrs. Frazier?"

The voice was so close that Janet jumped like a startled rabbit, dropping the flashlight as she spun around.

Rodney was leaning against the rear fender of his pickup truck watching her. He was dressed in jeans and a bright orange nylon windbreaker. The same shade as the frayed wind-sock, Janet thought incongruously. Except that his jacket was in considerably better shape.

"Or were you looking for something, Mrs. Frazier?" His mocking tone belied the polite words. "This is a strange place to find you."

"I'm not thrilled with it myself." She bent to retrieve the flashlight and made herself walk up to the car and toss it casually on the front seat. "I didn't pick the place. Your mother said I'd find you here."

"Thelma!" He stared at her incredulously, turning his back to the wind which was blowing his long hair across his face. "I don't believe it!"

"You'd better. I certainly wouldn't be here otherwise. Your wife came to the hotel and asked for help."

His hand clenched. "Hana shouldn't be driving around. The doctor told her to stay in bed. Otherwise, she'll lose the baby."

Janet felt sympathy for his obvious concern. "Well, she was all right when I left and your mother was caring for her. That's why I came to find you—there wasn't anyone else."

"So they sent you." He began to laugh silently, his drooping Fu-Manchu moustache looking even more grotesque as his lips moved. "God, that's rich!"

"I don't see what's so funny," she retorted sharply, puzzled by his sudden insolence. "Your family's sick with worry. I don't know what trouble you're in, but

# THE CAPTURED HEART

you're to get out while there's still time. Thelma said to tell you that she'll find another way."

"And you don't know what I'm involved in," he mimicked, ignoring her other words. "Like hell, you don't! I must say I admire your nerve, or"—his eyebrows drew together— "did you think you could cut in on the profits?"

"What are you talking about?" Janet's palms felt clammy with fear as she saw him straighten and move toward her. "I've told you the reason I'm here. All I want to do now is leave—you can take it from there."

"Not so fast." He brushed her hand roughly from the door handle of the car when she started to open it. "Alli!" he called commandingly.

Immediately the springs on the seat of the pickup cab creaked as a young Oriental girl sat up and opened the door. She moved faster when Rodney snapped at her again in an unknown dialect.

"What in the world . . ." Janet stared incredulously when the slight young woman, dressed in nondescript blue cotton pants and jacket, jumped to the ground and started to rummage in the flatbed of the truck. "Where did she come from? Honestly, Rodney, this is too much! If you could have seen your wife crying her heart out and all the while you've been flirting in the boondocks with another woman . . ."

Rodney's sudden guffaw made her break off. "You're good at it, Mrs. Frazier," he said grudgingly. "I'll hand it to you." Then he grunted with satisfaction as the Chinese girl sidled up beside him holding a length of dirty cord. He spat out another command to her, and before Janet could protest, the woman caught both her hands and was binding them behind her back.

"What are you doing? Stop that!" Janet pulled away, struggling frantically to free her wrists. She was brought up short by a brutal blow on the head from Rodney that made her senses reel. He held her against the car, still moaning with pain, while the Chinese girl finished tying her hands.

"It's your own damn fault, Mrs. Frazier. You should have stayed out of this from the beginning," Rodney told her callously when he'd checked her wrists to make sure the rope was tight enough. "Coming here now with some cock-and-bull story about Hana isn't going to change my mind. I suppose you overheard her talking to Thelma."

"I told you what happened," Janet's words sounded thick even to her own ears and she leaned her forehead against the top of the car door, hoping the contact with the metal surface would help her to think. Dimly she heard the Chinese girl question Rodney in an anxious tone. There was something familiar in her bearing, a mannerism distinctive enough to make Janet turn her head painfully and stare at her again. This time the girl stared defiantly back, as if to emphasize that the American woman was no longer a threat.

"I know you!" Janet said suddenly, caution forgotten in her astonishment. She switched her gaze to

Rodney. "It's our maid from the hotel. She doesn't speak English so I didn't recognize her voice before."

He gave a snort of derision. "The English language is not the be-all and end-all of linguistics, Mrs. Frazier—despite what you American tourists think. Alli and I have no trouble communicating." His eyes ran over the Chinese girl in an intimate way that showed what he meant.

"That's your business," Janet said stiffly. "I don't see what it has to do with me."

"I wondered the same thing when I saw you staring at Alli the day she got off the boat at the Kona pier. You remember, Mrs. Frazier"—his hand was playing absently with the zipper on his jacket—"it was the day you both arrived."

Janet's eyes widened with disbelief. "You're crazy. I was on the pier to meet . . ."

". . . Your husband," Rodney finished for her. "I know—I was watching you. And then you stared at Alli and asked me about her later in the car."

"But it was just idle curiosity. I couldn't remember where I'd seen her." Janet's gaze went imploringly to the Oriental girl who stood stiffly beside them, her thin figure looking almost wraithlike in the moonlight.

"I don't believe you," Rodney snapped. "It wasn't idle curiosity that had you asking Thelma about her later, too." His mouth twisted. "You about had my fat mama on the ropes she was so scared."

"Why? What did she have to do with it?"

"Because she slipped Alli into the job at the hotel, of course. Once you started making noises about your maid not speaking English, it was only a matter of time until the housekeeper and Wayne Marshall would start asking questions. That's when I decided to cool you off a little. Lucky for you that guy of yours came out to the pool."

Janet sagged visibly against the car. "It was *you* who tried to drown me." She closed her eyes and took a deep breath before opening them again. "All that over such a little thing!"

He swore violently and shook her hard. "Don't play so damned dumb. Getting Alli to the mainland means lots of money and that's just the beginning for me in this racket. There'll be plenty more to follow her." His black eyes swept Janet's pale features disdainfully. "One lousy woman like you isn't going to upset my plans. That's why I moved the barricade on the path at the Volcanoes. You wouldn't have gotten away that time if I'd had a minute or two more."

"I thought it was the Bristows."

"That cheap grifter! Not a chance. I got the lowdown on him from security at the hotel. The whole damned island police force is waiting for him to make a move once that Exhibit opens. They caught up with the bellhop he bribed to lift that insurance list of yours. Not that it hurts to have everybody's attention on something else. That's why Alli was sent across now—for our trial run."

"But if it wasn't for the Exhibit—what was it?"

# THE CAPTURED HEART

"I'll be damned, lady . . . you never give up!" Rodney shook his head in mock admiration. "Never mind—it'll give you something to think about on the trip."

Janet's head went up fast at that, bringing on a wave of pain that made her wince. "Where are you taking me?"

"Don't worry, it's going to be a short trip. You won't even have to pack."

"You're running an awful risk—by this time, half of Kaiulani knows I've come to meet you . . ."

He shrugged. "Let them. I don't plan to come back here anyway. After tonight, I'm handling arrangements at the other end. We've got another man to take care of things on the big island."

The sudden noise of a motor coming across the still air made him break off in mid-sentence. Alli's face brightened and she touched his arm before pointing toward the dark waters of Wainani Bay.

Janet's gaze followed theirs toward two bobbing lights obviously fixed atop the mast of a small boat approaching from the north. She frowned then and turned back to Rodney. "But Thelma said you were meeting a pilot."

"There are different kinds of pilots, Mrs. Frazier. I've never believed in telling a woman too much. It isn't my fault if my mama got the wrong idea. She doesn't know about the rock pier down there beyond the runway or the deep-water moorage either." He reached out to pull her roughly upright. "If you behave yourself, you won't have to find out how deep that water is. Not right now, anyway. In fact, you might be amusing to keep around for a while."

While he was going on, the Chinese girl was watching him with a frown. Now she broke in with a sharp spate of words which made his lips tighten with annoyance.

He listened to her diatribe just momentarily before he made a threatening gesture, causing her to break off in the middle. After that, he snapped an order which sent her quickly over to the fence. She maneuvered her slight figure through the loose wires and started at a dogtrot across the runway toward the approaching craft.

"Now it's your turn, Mrs. Frazier," Rodney said, putting a heavy hand on her shoulder.

He was clearly enjoying her discomfort, and Janet tried not to show how terrified she was. "Look, you've the wrong idea about this whole thing. Nothing will be helped by taking me along," she pleaded, trying to stall for time. After what he'd told her, she knew that if she set foot on the tiny boat which was even then approaching the rock inlet that it would be a one-way passage.

Rodney's next words confirmed it. "They won't be happy to have another passenger. But then, they wouldn't be happy if I left any bodies lying around here on the grass either." His mirthless smile showed. "This way, it's neater. Come on, I don't want to keep them waiting." His grip on Janet's shoulder tightened. She gasped with pain but stumbled beside him toward the fence because there was no alternative. Without the use of her hands, any kind of defense was impossible.

They were at the barbed wire when the sound of a car being driven hard down the dirt track behind them merged with the muffled chug of the trawler's engine as it maneuvered up to the rocky pier.

Rodney tried to look over his shoulder as he was stooping to get through the loose barbed-wire strands. In that instant when he was intent on avoiding the rusty wire, his clutch on Janet loosened.

It was the chance she had been waiting for. She lunged and sent him sprawling face-first into the rough turf on the other side of the fence.

For an agonizing moment, she felt the sharp barbs rake her upper body as she reeled against the wire. Then she pulled herself free and staggered, half-running, back toward the car.

At any instant, she expected to feel Rodney's hands on her back. She *did* hear his blast of profanity that mercifully faded under the squeal of car brakes being hastily applied.

Then she became aware of heavy footsteps pounding toward her, and panic rose to submerge all thoughts of reason. An instant later, she stumbled over a lava fissure in the ground. She tried desperately but unsuccessfully to keep her balance, before finally collapsing onto the brittle grass.

## Chapter Eight

Shock, physical pain, and a reluctance to return to reality masked the rest of her time at Wainani Bay.

There were some moments of lucidity but not enough for Janet to sort out the male figures that surrounded her and untied her hands. Another shadowy figure lifted her into a car. He tried to be gentle, but her lacerations from the barbed wire made her moan softly and her eyelids settled down again.

Full consciousness didn't return until later in a small, scrubbed room when she pushed a vial of aromatic spirits of ammonia away from her nose and sat up to rejoin the world. She stared in bewilderment at the gray-haired Hawaiian man in a white coat beside her and then focused on Wayne Marshall hovering in the background. "What happened?" were her first words.

# THE CAPTURED HEART

"Neat . . . but not original," Wayne said, grinning with relief. "I'd hoped for better from you."

"Nevertheless, we're glad to have you with us again. I'm Dr. Owene," the older man said, putting the ammonia aside. "You're in my clinic at Mahukona. Now I'd better clean up those abrasions and see if I can make you more comfortable." He turned his head to stare pointedly at Wayne. "If Mr. Marshall will excuse us . . ."

"Oh, sure thing," the other assured him. "I was just sticking around to see that Mrs. Frazier was okay so I could send the good word. I'll be right outside when you're finished," he assured Janet. "We'll go back to Kaiulani later if Dr. Owene gives the okay."

The possibility that she wouldn't be allowed to return to the hotel made Janet look more apprehensive than ever. Her wistfulness didn't escape the older man.

He turned to Wayne and shook his head. "Your bedside manner would never do, young man. Of course, Mrs. Frazier can go home. *If* you'll get out of here so I can treat her."

"I'm going. I'm going." Wayne nodded and made for the door.

"Send the nurse in while you're about it," the doctor instructed. "A couple more hands will speed this up."

A pleasant middle-aged nurse came in a few minutes later. She clucked sympathetically when she saw Janet's dirty face and disheveled clothing, but her dismay didn't keep her from efficiently assisting the doctor when he cleansed the scratches and bandaged them.

"It's a shame about this pretty dress," she remarked to Janet as she helped her slip back into it. "I'm afraid it's beyond repair."

"I know." Janet surveyed the ripped material ruefully. "Barbed wire didn't do a thing for it."

"Be glad that you're in better shape," Dr. Owene said over his shoulder as he straightened from washing his hands and reached for a paper towel. "I'm thankful those lacerations are shallow. There shouldn't be any trouble with the healing." He came back to where she was sitting. "How about the dizziness? Is that gone now?"

Janet stood up carefully and was happy to discover she was feeling better by the minute. "Yes, thanks, I'll be fine."

"I'm sure you will. Nevertheless, I'll call you tomorrow morning to double-check." He went over to the clinic door, which opened onto a broad porch. "Now where did Marshall go? Ah . . . there he is in the parking lot. He's heading this way."

"There's no need. I can meet him by the car." Janet smiled as she shook hands. "Thank you both. You were so kind."

"Just take care of yourself and we'll be repaid," the doctor said. "Watch those steps now."

"I will. Good night." Janet waved and threaded her way through the rows of cars which filled the parking lot. For an instant she wondered what attracted all the people and then she noticed that the building flanking Dr. Owene's clinic was a busy restaurant.

"How about this for timing?" Wayne caught up with her by the back bumper of his car. "Go ahead and get in."

She went obediently around and slid onto the front seat. Then she smiled as she saw two steaming cups on the glove compartment. "Coffee! It smells wonderful!"

"I decided we needed some additional therapy." Wayne got in behind the steering wheel and slammed his door. "Coffee never goes amiss and I didn't think you'd feel like sitting in the restaurant." He handed her a styrofoam cup. "That's for you—I put sugar in mine."

She shook her head in silent admiration. "All this and a talented publicity man, too. I'm impressed."

"So am I. Just shows what a woman's influence can do to a man. There's no need to look alarmed," he went on with a grin, "I'm all set to be a friend of the family. Especially since that husband of yours is stiff-necked about anything else."

Janet took a swallow of coffee and leaned back against the seat. "Does Scott know what happened tonight?" she asked carefully.

Wayne choked violently on a mouthful of the hot liquid. It took a half minute of coughing and wiping his eyes before he was able to answer.

"Who in the dickens do you think organized this

bun fight? You husband would be here now except that I knew where the doctor hung out. Besides, the two policemen with us needed all the help they could get when they took out after Rodney. I was odd man out," he concluded grimly. "Once Scott put you in the car I didn't have a chance to argue. That guy has a way of giving orders." He shook his head.

"I know." Janet's voice was full of feeling. She sat quietly for a moment trying to catalogue her thoughts. Apparently Scott was still taking care of his responsibilities. She should have known that he would have come after her. Dared to have more faith. She glanced down into the coffee cup and swirled the liquid absently.

"Your coffee's getting cold." Wayne was watching her thoughtful profile. "Drink it—you still look pale. Did that damned Rodney . . ."

She shook her head hastily. "He didn't have a chance. But if you hadn't come when you did . . ."

"No use thinking about that. Scott's friend from police headquarters in Hilo showed up at Kaiulani with another officer right after you drove off. When you had that trouble at the Volcanoes, he had started nosing into Rodney's record as well as the Bristows'. He discovered that Rodney was in deep with the moneylenders but that he'd promised a big pay-off soon. The Hilo police thought that warranted a personal call on Mr. Kahori. When they got to the hotel, they found Scott ready to take out after you." Wayne gave her a rueful smile. "After you had turned up missing, your husband came to me . . . I can't imagine why that man's so suspicious."

Janet's lips curved in response. "Don't change the subject. What happened then?"

"Well, Thelma came in about the time I was claiming the Fifth Amendment and told us what had happened. She'd been worried about sending you to Wainani after she'd heard more of the story from Rodney's wife. Thelma claims she didn't realize how deeply he was involved."

"I can believe that." Janet finished the coffee and put the empty plastic cup by her feet. "Actually, I feel sorry for her."

"Now that it's over, maybe." Wayne finished his own coffee. "Right then, I think Scott could have gone after her with a baseball bat. She *did* give us directions about where you'd gone. The next thing I knew, I was in the back seat of a police car with Scott. He was giving those two officers hell for not going faster. Talk about flying low! I'm too old for that stuff."

"That makes two of us." She watched as he switched on the ignition and drove carefully out of the parking lot. "But did you ever find out what Rodney was involved in? He kept talking about that Chinese maid." She saw the puzzled frown he shot her and went on to explain quickly. "The girl on our floor. Thelma can tell you about her."

Wayne grimaced and smacked his forehead with the heel of his palm. "Now it makes sense. The police mentioned something about the smuggling of illegal aliens from Red China. They've been shipped over to the outer islands in considerable numbers recently. Hawaii was the place to indoctrinate them. You know, language, clothes, that sort of stuff. Afterwards they could be safely put on a plane for the mainland with a fake passport."

Janet whistled silently. "Rodney was playing for high stakes. There must be a lot of people involved." She half-turned to face him. "But we don't even know if they caught Rodney or the girl. And the crew of that trawler wouldn't have just stood around waiting to be captured."

"Stop worrying," Wayne told her. "Those two policemen were big bruisers and that husband of yours can certainly take care of himself."

"I hope so. It's awful . . . not knowing."

"Look, we'll be back at the hotel in a half hour. The best thing you can do is lean back and relax. It won't help Scott a bit if you have a relapse."

Janet bit her lip as she thought it over. "I suppose you're right." Then she gestured apologetically. "I'm sorry. I haven't even thanked you for what you've done. It couldn't have been fun for you taking care of the 'walking wounded.' You'd probably rather have been in the thick of it, too."

He grinned companionably. "This had its compensations. You're quite a gal. If you ever decide to leave home . . ."

"I'll keep it in mind." She was glad that Wayne

# THE CAPTURED HEART

couldn't see her features as she leaned back in the shadowed interior of the car. She certainly wasn't going to confess to him that Hawaii would be the last place she'd ever come when she and Scott finally extricated themselves from this ridiculous marriage. Now she only had to wait until the Exhibit was opened before she could go back to New York and start the proceedings for a quick divorce.

She turned to stare out the car window, blinking to keep the tears in her eyes from spilling over. It was just the aftermath of all that had happened, she told herself fiercely. The hopelessness of loving Scott had nothing to do with it.

The worst part of the whole affair was that she felt so foolish. She hadn't asked to care for the man—hadn't even wanted to. Now his image would haunt her for the rest of her life.

From the corner of his eye, Wayne saw her search for a handkerchief and blow her nose. She was still suffering from shock, he decided, and hoped Scott Frazier would know what to do. He thought of saying something but changed his mind when Janet turned her head to stare out the side window again. Instead, he pressed down more firmly on the accelerator. As the speedometer needle soared, he hoped the two policemen from Hilo were still too busy to bother with little matters like speeding tickets.

Janet had her emotions under firm control when they finally drove into the curving entrance of Kaiulani. Even before the doorman had opened the car door for her, she was able to turn to Wayne with a smile and thank him. "You were wonderful. I'll never forget how kind you've been." Then, leaning forward swiftly, she kissed him on the corner of the mouth and got out of the car before he could respond.

"Dirty pool." He grinned and shook his head, secretly relieved that she seemed back to normal. "No fair when I can't reciprocate."

"I know." She managed to keep her tone light as she started to walk away. "See you at the Exhibit in the morning."

Wayne's expression sobered when he watched her move swiftly into the lighted lobby. The news he'd been told after telephoning the police from Mahukona had been sketchy. Too inconclusive to worry Janet with it. He sighed as he pulled the car around to park it at the end of the drive. By now, it should be resolved one way or another.

Janet let herself into her hotel room and looked around expectantly. Her face fell on seeing the deserted premises; it hadn't occurred to her that Scott wouldn't be there waiting. She dropped her purse on the closest bed as she walked over to the lanai doors and slid them open. Outside, the deserted lounge and clean ashtray on the table gave mute evidence that her husband hadn't been there recently either.

For the first time, the possibility that Scott could have come to harm came surging to the fore in her mind. Now that she thought of it, Wayne hadn't been particularly reassuring. It was more than possible that

## THE CAPTURED HEART

all three men could have been injured trying to board that trawler.

She stood clutching the lanai door with fingers suddenly moist with nervousness. There was also the chance that Scott and the police were still searching for the trawler in the offshore waters. In that case, Rodney and the girl could have doubled back looking for a place to hide. Thelma or even Hana could have been forced to cover for them. Until she found out, she'd better make sure all doors were locked. Afterwards, she'd call the police.

Purposefully she secured the catch on the lanai and had moved halfway across the bedroom to lock the hall door when an unidentified sound stopped her in her tracks. She remained frozen in the middle of the floor for fully a minute. Then, just when she had convinced herself it had been her imagination, the sound came again. This time there was no doubt that it originated beyond the closed bathroom door.

Her first instinct was to dash out into the corridor. If she could get to the lobby and call for help, there might be time . . .

Her thoughts surged frantically and she pressed her temples with shaking fingers. This wouldn't do! She had to stop being such a ninny and use her head. A sane woman didn't go shrieking to the lobby when there could be a logical explanation for a noise in the next room. All she had to do was open the door and discover the cause.

Slowly, she took a step that way. Then another . . .

as she told herself reassuringly it could be the maid. Another maid, she corrected hastily before her fears rose to swamp her.

Suddenly the thought occurred to her that it could be Scott. He could have been hurt . . . could be lying on the floor now. Rodney could have come back to the hotel for cover and caught him unaware . . .

Without stopping to think again, she ran the last few steps to the bathroom door and thrust it open.

The scene that met her eyes was so unbelievable that she could only stand gasping on the threshold as she tried to take it in.

Scott was not lying bleeding on the floor. Nor was he on the deck of a dirty trawler somewhere on the choppy ocean. Instead he was lying on his back in the middle of a calm bathtub . . . her bathtub . . . obviously enjoying the hot water and—her nose twitched angrily as a faint pine odor wafted toward her—her bubble bath as well.

He brought his head up calmly from the layer of froth to survey her without surprise. "I was wondering when you'd get here," he remarked.

That dispassionate, couldn't-care-less statement was the final indignity. The last shreds of Janet's self-control simply self-destructed.

Hands on hips, she advanced toward him like a tornado swooping in from the East China Sea. "You wondered when I'd get here," she mimicked in acid tones. "That was kind of you. I'm surprised you could fit it in. All this time I've been wondering whether you were lying unconscious on the deck of that damned boat or whether you'd been fed to the sharks an hour ago." She took another step closer to the tub. "I even wondered whether you were still lying out on that miserable runway bleeding into the grass. That was before it occurred to me that Rodney could have escaped and come back here to hit you over the head." As he frowned and started to sit up, she put up a hand. "No—don't stir yourself now. It's a little late to observe any of the decencies—like letting me know you were all right." Her voice gathered momentum. "Or being in the bedroom when I came back so you wouldn't scare me half to death making noises like some damned porpoise in the bathtub. I suppose that was asking too much." She was shouting then . . . knowing she was doing it . . . and delighting in every appalling syllable. "Not only that"—she was casting about for anything to continue the tirade since she was running out of ammunition and hated to quit—"you even took my bubble bath! Well, I hope you choke on it." She snatched up the plastic bottle from the edge of the tub and, without thinking, dumped the rest of the green mixture over his shoulders.

There was an instant of suspended animation as Scott's jaw dropped open. As if he couldn't believe what was happening. Then, as she flipped the empty container into the tub and turned to flee, he submerged once, sending a layer of suds cascading over the sides of the porcelain tub before he rose like a mighty Phoenix intent on resurrection.

Janet didn't linger to see. She took to her heels and fled to the hall door. As her hand clutched the knob, she remembered that she'd need money for her escape. Even feminine pride didn't make an adequate substitute for a well-filled wallet. She turned and dived for the satin pouch bag in the middle of the bedspread.

This proved a fatal mistake in tactics.

Scott, bundling his length in a terry robe, catapulted through the bathroom door and caught her by the arm. His momentum brought them up short at the edge of the bed. For a second, they both strove to regain their balance and then, gravity won, and they sprawled onto the yielding mattress.

"Let me go!" Janet struggled to free herself, pounding ineffectually against his broad chest. "Let me *go*, I tell you . . ."

"The hell I will! I warned you what would happen the next time you tried that." He caught a hank of her flaming hair and pulled her chin up to kissing range. "New rules, honey, and a different playground." His other hand ran possessively down her soft, curved figure which was molded to his. "And if you only knew how long I've been waiting to get you on this playground . . ." His voice trailed off as his mouth moved to fasten on her parted lips as if he'd never let them go.

After that, neither of them could have told how

much time passed. Life became an enchanted interlude bounded by their embrace. People in love know there is no real way to measure the height of passion any more than the depths of despair. Scott and Janet did know that their struggle was over—finally and irrevocably. And, with rare mortal wisdom, accorded the culmination of their love the proper awe and respect.

It was much later that they surveyed each other with newfound knowledge and bemusement. Scott shifted to a more comfortable position and pushed the pillow around so that they could both use it. "Now, Madam Frazier," he smiled as her cheeks flooded with color at the term, "just for the record, I'd like to announce that I was unfairly accused a while ago." His arm tightened possessively around her shoulders. "You little idiot! Wayne called me from Mahukona while you were with the doctor. I asked him to."

Her bewildered gaze came up in surprise. "Then why didn't he tell me?"

"Because I told him not to." His voice sobered. "Rodney was injured in the fracas on the boat. His head hit a steel capstan . . . they don't know whether he'll come out of it."

She winced. "Poor Thelma. And poor Hana . . . with the baby coming."

"I know. One of the policemen got a torn hand out of the fight and I collected some bruises trying to persuade the captain not to put out to sea. That's why I was soaking in that damned tub."

"Darling, you didn't tell me."

He broke into unrestrained laughter. "You didn't give me a chance. I thought for a minute you were going to drown me before I could get out of the water." His eyes kindled as he stared down at her embarrassed features. "The trouble I'm letting myself in for. Imagine keeping that redheaded temper of yours under control for the rest of my life."

Her hesitant glance sought his. "You're sure you want to? I haven't forgotten how you were shanghaied into this."

His lips moved softly over her delicately curved brow. "Honey, *nobody* shanghais a grown man into standing in front of a minister these days unless he has a few ideas of his own. I've been sending up thanks to Madame Pele ever since I saw you on the Kona pier."

"And I thought I was going to have to go back home alone," she murmured, finding enough courage to tell the truth.

He shook his head emphatically. "There was never a chance, angel. I fell in love with you then, I've loved you ever since, and I haven't the slightest doubt that I'm going to remain in the same pitiful state for the next fifty years or so. Now . . ." his eyes darkened as they swept over the soft, feminine curves beside him, "the defense rests. I think we could find more interesting things to talk about . . . or do."

"Very possibly." The way her lips traced a soft line along his jaw and nuzzled the lobe of his ear showed

# THE CAPTURED HEART

that he wouldn't meet any real argument on that score. But when he started to pull her more tightly against him, he felt her quiver with sudden laughter.

His eyebrows went up. "Now what, my love?"

"I was just thinking." Amusement gleamed in her lovely blue eyes. "Sometime before morning, we'll have to remember to go over and muss up that other bed."

He grinned. "Why? Kaiulani's a honeymoon hotel. The help's used to things like that."

"Maybe. But I'm taking no chances. The new maid will speak English, don't forget." Her hands stole around his neck to caress the back of his head. "But there's lots of time."

"No hurry at all, dearest." He bent over her again and this time met no resistance. "Remind me again in the morning."

# Glenna Finley

Glenna Finley is a native of Washington State. She earned her degree from Stanford University in Russian Studies and in Speech and Dramatic Arts, with emphasis on radio.

After a stint in radio and publicity work in Seattle, she went to New York City to work for NBC as a producer in its international division. In addition, she worked with the "March of Time" and *Life* magazine.

As a producer, she had her own show about activities in Manhattan, a show that was broadcast to England. The programs were similar to those of the "Voice of America."

Though her life in New York was exciting, she eventually returned to the Northwest where she married. Currently residing in Seattle with her husband Donald Witte and their sons, she loves to travel, and draws heavily on her travels and experiences for the novels that have been published. Her books for NAL have sold several million copies.

## SIGNET Romances You'll Enjoy Reading

- ☐ **WHO IS LUCINDA?** by **Hermina Black.** Her past was buried in memory. Could she trust this new love that wanted to claim her future? (#Q6247—95¢)

- ☐ **VENETIAN INHERITANCE** by **Annette Eyre.** She was caught in the legacy of a forbidden love. . . .
  (#Q6524—95¢)

- ☐ **DANGEROUS MASQUERADE** by **Hermina Black.** It started as an amusing charade of love. But soon her happiness became the stake in a perilous game of hearts. (#Q6228—95¢)

- ☐ **THE ROOTS OF LOVE** by **Vivian Donald.** For the first time published in this country, popular British writer Vivian Donald has written a gripping story of love and mystery in the Highlands of Scotland. (#T6043—75¢)

- ☐ **DANGER IN MONTPARNASSE** by **Hermina Black.** When a sinister figure from the past suddenly reappeared, Fiona realized with chilling terror that she was being used as a pawn in a perilous charade of love and deception. Would her new-found love, who had rescued her once, be there when she needed him again?
  (#Q5877—95¢)

- ☐ **THE BECKONING DREAM** by **Evelyn Berckman.** Ann longed to reach out to the man she had fallen so desperately in love with, but another woman prevented her —an unscrupulous woman who knew the secret behind the haunting, recurrent dream that threatened to destroy Ann's life. (#Q5997—95¢)

---

**THE NEW AMERICAN LIBRARY, INC.,**
P.O. Box 999, Bergenfield, New Jersey 07621

Please send me the SIGNET BOOKS I have checked above. I am enclosing $_____ (check or money order—no currency or C.O.D.'s). Please include the list price plus 25¢ a copy to cover handling and mailing costs. (Prices and numbers are subject to change without notice.)

Name_____

Address_____

City_____ State_____ Zip Code_____

Allow at least 3 weeks for delivery

## Have You Read These Bestsellers from SIGNET?

☐ **JENNIE, VOLUME I: The Life of Lady Randolph Churchill by Ralph G. Martin.** In JENNIE, Ralph G. Martin creates a vivid picture of an exciting woman, Lady Randolph Churchill, who was the mother of perhaps the greatest statesman of this century, Winston Churchill, and in her own right, one of the most colorful and fascinating women of the Victorian era. (#J6600—$1.95)

☐ **JENNIE, VOLUME II: The Life of Lady Randolph Churchill, the Dramatic Years 1895–1921 by Ralph G. Martin.** The climactic years of scandalous passion and immortal greatness of the American beauty who raised a son to shape history, Winston Churchill. "An extraordinary lady ... if you couldn't put down JENNIE ONE, you'll find JENNIE TWO just as compulsive reading!"—*Washington Post* (#E5196—$1.75)

☐ **ELIZABETH AND CATHERINE by Robert Coughlan.** For the millions enthralled by Nicholas & Alexandra, the glittering lives and loves of the two Russian Empresses who scandalized the world and made a nation ... "Fascinating!"—*The Boston Globe*. A Putnam Award Book and a Literary Guild Featured Alternate.
(#J6455—$1.95)

☐ **PENTIMENTO by Lillian Hellman.** Hollywood in the days of Sam Goldwyn ... New York in the glittering times of Dorothy Parker and Tallulah Bankhead ... a 30-year love affair with Dashiell Hammett, and a distinguished career as a playwright. "Exquisite ... brilliantly finished ... it will be a long time before we have another book of personal reminiscence as engaging as this one."—*New York Times Book Review* (#J6091—$1.95)

---

**THE NEW AMERICAN LIBRARY, INC.,**
P.O. Box 999, Bergenfield, New Jersey 07621

Please send me the SIGNET BOOKS I have checked above. I am enclosing $_____ (check or money order—no currency or C.O.D.'s). Please include the list price plus 25¢ a copy to cover handling and mailing costs. (Prices and numbers are subject to change without notice.)

Name_____

Address_____

City_____ State_____ Zip Code_____

Allow at least 3 weeks for delivery